Loving Chloe

CHRIS KENISTON
USA TODAY BESTSELLING AUTHOR

Indie House Publishing

Indie House Publishing

BOOKS BY CHRIS KENISTON

Hart Land
Heather
Lily
Violet
Iris
Hyacinth
Rose
Calytrix
Zinnia
Poppy

Farraday Country
Adam
Brooks
Connor
Declan
Ethan
Finn
Grace
Hannah
Ian
Jamison
Keeping Eileen
Loving Chloe
Morgan

Aloha Series Heartwarming Edition
Aloha Texas
Almost Paradise
Mai Tai Marriage
Dive Into You

Look of Love
Love by Design
Love Walks In
Flirting with Paradise

Surf's Up Flirts
(Aloha Series Companions)
Shall We Dance
Love on Tap
Head Over Heels
Perfect Match
Just One Kiss
It Had to Be You

**Other Books
By Chris Keniston**

Honeymoon Series
Honeymoon for One
Honeymoon for Three
Honeymoon for Four

Family Secrets Novels
Champagne Sisterhood
The Homecoming
Hope's Corner

Original Aloha Series
Waikiki Wedding

ACKNOWLEDGEMENTS

Well, y'all asked for a Farraday holiday and you got it!

Had to scramble like heck, and for that I have to thank all my author friends who came to my rescue when I got stuck: Elle James, Wendy Lester, Dale Mayer, Barb Han, and Kathy Ivan. Sometimes I wonder who actually writes these books. LOL.

I want to thank all my readers for loving the Farradays as much as I do and for patiently waiting for more. I may have a few surprises for you ☐

An extra thanks to my daughter for her support this last month in helping me manage my time and my new grandbaby and still write this novella. You rock sweetie!

CHAPTER ONE

Little in life could beat a west Texas sunrise. Mingling of reds, oranges, yellows, and pinks created a kaleidoscope of color to energize even the most tired of souls. And this morning Officer Reed Taylor was tired.

The holiday season was in full swing, and as much as Christmas brought out the best in most people, it brought out the crazy in others. One hour left in the graveyard shift at the Tuckers Bluff PD, and after chasing a merry band of teenage pranksters out tipping cows from the one end of the Farraday spread to the north side of the Brady's, he felt like his shift had gone on for days not hours.

Reed could only hope, with the grace of God, the good people of Tuckers Bluff would refrain from any more mischief until it was DJ's turn to deal with it. He glanced at the dashboard; in fifty-four minutes he'd be on his way home and could sleep till his new neighbor's crazy mixed up rooster crowed at the setting sun. That thought made him smile.

It had been a big decision to stop renting and buy his own place here in Tuckers Bluff. Even bigger to choose a home outside of the city limits. Close enough to reach the police station quickly if needed, but far enough away that the quiet sounds of country living lulled him to sleep like a newborn in his mama's arms. And if he were honest, deep enough in Farraday country to be included in weekly Sunday suppers. The Marine Corps had made him and DJ brothers. Aunt Eileen, Sean, and every other member of the clan had made him family.

"Reed," Esther's voice came through the radio squawk, "are you on your way back in yet?"

"10-4," he replied.

"I just got a call from Nadine Peabody. Says there's a coyote in her yard making her cats nervous."

Reed chuckled to himself. Nadine Peabody was quite the character. Indulging a lonely old woman's need for a little human contact and conversation was considerably easier than the things that might have sprung up when he and DJ were cops in Dallas. "On my way."

"Copy that."

Arriving at Nadine's would take about thirty minutes. The trick would be escaping in less than twenty for the end of his shift. His cell phone buzzed and he wondered who was calling at this hour. "Hello."

"Hey, man. Are you anywhere near the ranch?" DJ asked.

"Sorry. Already passed it. What's up?"

"Nothing much. Jamison wants Aunt Eileen's ginormous corned beef pot and I thought if I could catch you it would save me a trip."

"I can turn around if you want. Only thing pending is Nadine Peabody and a stalking coyote." He could almost hear DJ rolling his eyes. The coyote was most likely merely another figment of the creative and slightly paranoid woman's imagination. She practically lived at his brother Brooks' veterinary clinic. If there was such a thing as a cat hypochondriac, that was Nadine. Though the whole town knew most of it was just a need to talk.

"Tell you what. You go get the pot and I'll take care of Nadine."

"Sounds like a plan." The rising sun bounced off a large gray hump in the middle of the road.

"What the heck?" Slowing down, the now two gray humps came more clearly into view.

"What's wrong?" DJ's voice dropped to a concerned low.

"Not sure." First thought might have been Nadine's coyotes had high-tailed it west, but these roadblocks were a tad too large for a coyote. More likely… "Looks like Gray and his lady friend are out for a stroll."

"How far did you say you are from the ranch?"

"Four, maybe five miles."

"Odd," DJ mumbled. "Since the tornado those two stick close to Dad and Aunt Eileen."

"Well, right now they've taken to sightseeing dead center of the road."

"Sightseeing?"

"Just standing there staring at me like they've seen the second coming." The sun lifting higher in the sky, he killed the lights and came to a stop yards from the statuesque canines.

"Are you sure it's our dogs? *The* dogs?" There was no missing the incredulity in DJ's tone. The guy may have trusted Reed with his life a time or two, but DJ clearly thought he'd lost his eyesight now.

"I'm telling you… wait." Almost as though reassured they'd made eye contact, the two still animals turned away from the road. "They're on the move."

"Now that sounds more like them." A sharp howl pierced the country quiet. "Is that Gray?"

"It's one of them." The two had stopped across the road, and this time the other dog lifted his muzzle to the air and let out another sharp howl before turning and once again racing away from the road.

Shaking his head, Reed slowly pulled onto the shoulder, spinning the steering wheel to return to the Farraday ranch. "On my way for the pot."

As quickly as the adopted Farraday dogs had appeared in the road ahead, the two sat once again in his path. How the hell did they do that? Another howl and icy fingers skittered up his back and his gut sent out an alert. Something was up, and he knew deep down it wasn't good. "I'd swear they expect me to follow."

Showing no signs of being alarmed by the odd behavior, DJ chuckled into the phone. "You never know with those two."

He wished he found the dogs behavior as amusing as DJ. "I'm pulling over. Getting a closer look at what's going on." One foot out the door, the animals bolted away from him, barking and running toward a wisp of gray dusting the brightening, pristine skyline. "Oh, hell!"

"What?" All humor had fallen away from DJ's tone.

"Smoke."

"How bad?"

"Better have Esther sound the alarm. North of the main road, five miles east of the ranch. The pot will have to wait. I'm on my way."

"Ten four."

Reed's gut did a back flip. Only two possibilities in this direction. One of the Bradys had a small spread between the Farraday ranch and town. And then Chloe. *Damn.* Soon half the county would be descending on the volunteer station, but this far out of town it was up to the rancher—or widow—to control the burn.

Never before had he prayed so hard for the culprit to be a potentially catastrophic brush fire. Chloe didn't need this. The dogs had disappeared into the pasture, but it made no difference, they'd alerted him to the fire. He reached for his cell and managed to scroll to Farraday.

Within seconds Aunt Eileen was on the other end.

"There's smoke due east of you," he said in a rush. "We could use your water trucks."

"East. Bradys?"

He'd gone far enough to track the source. "Not that far."

"Chloe." Aunt Eileen's words dripped with the same concern licking at his nerves.

The tiny clapboard house on the small plot of land in the middle of what most folks considered nowhere was a bargain for his buddy Pat. His little piece of heaven. *Damn.*

"I'll alert Sean and Finn. The Bradys too. Consider us on our way."

The call disconnected before he could grunt a response. He could have used Aunt Eileen in the Marine Corps.

By the time he'd reached the gateless dirt road ahead, there wasn't any doubt. The wisp of gray plumes suddenly grew dark and thick. Reed's stomach turned and he floored the gas pedal, flying over pot holes like Wylie Coyote chasing the Roadrunner. Except this was one race he couldn't afford to lose.

• • • •

What in the name of all the heavens was that noise? Chloe Landon opened one eye. The sun was barely peeking through the blinds. According to the clock at her bedside, she had at least another hour before the girls awakened. It had taken just about all of Sarah's two plus years to train her not to rise with the roosters. Not that she had any roosters, but this morning it sounded like a flock of nature's alarm clock was scratching at her window.

Flinging the covers to one side, a loud bark broke the morning silence. Before her sleep-webbed brain could process the possibilities or her feet touched the floor, the sound of glass shattering filled the air.

"What the …" A gray bullet the size of a cannon shot toward her. Fear quickly pricked at her spine, her arm had already fumbled at the locked drawer where Pat had insisted she keep a gun when he wasn't home. *"Not that I expect trouble here,"* he'd say, but *you can't be too sure."*

A bark pierced the memory and large, very sharp, and very pointy teeth latched onto the sleeve of the hand still fumbling with the locked drawer. Her heart lurched in her chest but, rather than gnaw on her for breakfast, the animal hopped off the bed and tugged her to the floor with him.

"Chloe?" The distant voice sounded frantic. "Chloe." There was no mistaking the desperation in the rapid fire of her name. Or the voice. Reed. What the heck was he doing in her house, and at this hour?

The dog let go of her arm and circling around, nudged at her from the rear, almost toppling her forward. Another voice, a man's voice, echoed Reed. Her mouth dropped open to shout only to have the dog bark instead, then snap at her nightgown in another effort to drag her forward.

"Her room is down this hall," Reed shouted. "I'll get the girls."

Her girls! Like her husband had, she'd trust her life to Reed, but none of this made sense. Maneuvering around the dog hell bent on moving her in the opposite direction, she bolted towards her door as the stubborn animal leaned into her, shoving her toward the shards of broken glass scattered before her bedroom window.

"Chloe." Sean Farraday came bursting through her door. "We have to get you out. Now."

"What's going on?" She batted at the dog once again grabbing for her skirt. Not till the patriarch's strong hands grabbed her waist throwing her over his shoulder did she smell the smoke billowing into her room behind him. *Smoke*. Her girls! Pushing against a rock hard chest with all she had, she pounded on the man. "Put me down! The girls are upstairs."

Never in her life did she think she would have to fight a man as nice as Sean Farraday when still holding her tight, he sprinted over the glass.

"Reed's on it. We need to get you out."

Words and air battled in her throat. "Emmie, Sarah," she muttered as Sean shoved her, bottom first, out the window and into waiting arms.

Strong arms circled around her. "The sooner you stop kicking me, the sooner I can help Reed with the girls."

It took a moment to process she was now battling Finn Farraday with the same force she'd beaten on his father.

"Anyone else inside beside the girls?" Finn asked.

She shook her head. Words still weren't coming. She had to get back inside. Upstairs. *The girls*!

"The stairs are blocked." Sean Farraday practically flew out the window and without breaking stride, ran around her house.

"Ma'am, you have to promise me you'll stay here." Finn

looked totally torn between hanging onto her and bolting after his father. "We need water and I can't do both."

Her gaze shifted to the huge pickup truck with a massive water tank in the back and then she made the critical mistake of looking up. Orange flames shot through the roof. Her house – her girls—were on fire.

• • • •

By the time Reed reached the inside of Chloe's house, the flames had already swallowed the living room, robbing him of precious time. There was no way he could be in two ends of the house at once, and no way did he want to choose between saving Chloe or her daughters. Never had he been so thankful to see Sean Farraday come barreling through a doorway.

Confident that Chloe would be safe with the Farraday patriarch, he tore up the steps two a time. The heat on his back was scorching and the hardwood steps beneath his feet sank like sponge. Untucking the tail of his shirt, he raised it over his mouth. He had to get to the girls. This had to be a rescue. He could only hope that more help was on the way and fast, because there wasn't a doubt in his mind he was not getting those two girls out of the house the same way he'd come in.

The closer he got to the opposite end of the second floor hallway, the harder moving forward became. The smoke had grown thick and black and he'd resorted to feeling his way down the hall, counting the doors, thanking God he didn't feel the heat of burning flames through the walls. Though he rarely had reason to go upstairs, he did remember the second floor had two bedrooms, Chloe's beloved walk-in Christmas closet that had made her giddy with delight the first time Pat had shown her the house, and a bathroom. Only one more door.

Heat from below seeped through the floors. His feet might as well have been on fire. Maybe they were. No time to think. Adrenaline coursed through his system. He couldn't let Chloe down.

The few short steps to what should be the last door, Reed didn't bother feeling for the heat. Whatever was on the other side, so were Emmie and Sarah. The palm of his hand stung as he turned the knob and shoved the door open, slamming it shut behind him. Nothing. He couldn't see a damn thing. Down on all fours, he shouted for the girls and coughed on the smoke. Nothing.

"Emmie!" he choked. Silence. Damn.

The crashing sound of glass shattered the dread threatening to overtake him. This had to be a rescue, he silently repeated. Water poured in. Help had arrived. If they knew which room to douse, then Chloe must have told them which was the girls' room. Chloe had to be okay. The moment of relief passed too quickly to relish. *The girls.*

At this point, if not for the water gushing in the window, he wouldn't know which end was which in the room. "Emmie!" he called out again. This time he thought he'd heard a tiny sound. Scurrying toward the window and the single bed, he flung his hands across the top. Empty. It would probably be too much to hope a five and two year old would have gone low and under the bed. Calling their names again and waving his arms, his heart sank just a bit to search underneath and come up empty again.

Another bed. There was another bed in the room, but not another sound.

"Reed!" Connor Farraday called to him from the window. "You got the girls?"

"No!"

"Damn," the neighboring Farraday muttered. "I'm coming in."

"Hang on," Reed called back. His knee had slammed into a hard surface. The footboard of the second bed. Repeating the same searching move he'd done with the other bed, Reed's heart finally did a quickstep. A massive lump lie under the covers. He prayed to God there were two little girls breathing clean air underneath. "Emmie!"

A small voice drifted out from an opening at the top of the sheets. "Uncle Reed?"

Emmie. "Yes, honey. Is Sarah with you?"

He wasn't totally sure, but he was willing to bet Emmie had just nodded at him.

At this point he couldn't see his hands in front of his own face. Pulling at Emmie, placing her over his shoulder and keeping some of the covers over her body, he felt the tug from beside her. Yes! "Over here!" he called to Connor.

The room barely had enough space to hold two beds and a dresser, but his voice was the only thing that would give Connor direction.

"The guys are doing their best," Connor held his arms out, "but we need to boogie. The place is crumbling."

Handing the older of the two girls to his friend, Reed nodded and snuggled Sarah close against him. A single thin blanket covered her, the only protection he had for the young child. The window only steps away, as Connor's head descended on the opposite side of the missing glass, the vise squeezing his heart eased a fraction. Another few moments and both of Chloe's girls would be safe. The roar of commotion outside carried up to him. Chloe's voice frantically screaming for her child as Connor reached the ground with Emmie.

Underneath his feet, the floorboards rumbled, a roar reached his ears and he knew. Time had just run out. The boom that followed blew the door off the hinges and the consuming flames burst inside chasing them like the hounds of hell. Heaven help him, he had no choice. Thrust forward the last step, he managed one word. "Catch!"

CHAPTER TWO

How How did this happen? On the tailgate of a Farraday pickup, Chloe sat huddled under a blanket with her two daughters pressed against her. *Now what?*

"I do wish you'd drink a little tea." Sissy and her sister stood side by side, lips pressed tightly together, their gazes settling on the sleeping children snuggled under Chloe's arms.

"I'm fine, thank you." Not that she really believed she was fine, but through the years of Pat's deployments, and then months that rolled into years after his death, she'd almost begun to believe the empty words. *Until now.*

"Thank heaven Reed wasn't on the other end of the county this morning." Sister, the sibling from the general store that reminded Chloe of everything good about the 1950's—well, maybe not so much the beehive hairdo—had given voice to the same thing Chloe had thought since being told how the morning had unfolded.

Half the town had come to fight the fire. The flames that had consumed her precious little house. Her gaze shifted to the tall man striding in her direction. Like everyone else who had come to do battle with the elements, Reed was soaked to the core and covered in soot. He'd saved her. Again.

"It was the tree, wasn't it?" she muttered softly.

Reed shook his head. "They don't think so."

"I'm going to run and see if the men need something more to drink." Sissy, the redhead, taller and leaner of the two siblings, elbowed her sister.

"Oh, yes," Sister squeaked. "I'll check the coolers."

Not till the two women had disappeared from view did Chloe dare speak. "What was it?"

Reed shut his eyes a moment and then blowing out a sigh, declared, "The heater. Too many things plugged into one outlet. The circuit couldn't handle it."

The old furnace. They'd managed to keep it going with spit, duct tape and a prayer since buying the house, but last year it had finally given up the ghost. Space heaters had been the perfect temporary solution for her struggling budget. At least she had thought so at the time.

"I'm sorry." His gaze fell to the two sleeping children.

She could see the pain and sincerity behind Reed's words. More than once he'd offered to replace the old heating system. If not a gift then a loan, he'd said. She had been too proud to accept. She'd asked herself would Pat have accepted? Not sure, she'd repeatedly said no thank you. Somehow she would make things work on her own. Now look at what her misplaced pride had cost her family.

"It's not your fault," she whispered. She knew as surely as she blamed herself that right this moment Reed was doing the same thing. "We're not your responsibility."

How many times had she said that and yet, the man didn't look any more convinced of it now than he had the last time or the time before that. She sort of understood, Semper Fi and all the brotherhood stuff, but she didn't know how to convince Reed or DJ that she and the girls weren't their problem. Letting her gaze drift to the charred structure that used to be her home, she didn't have a clue what would happen now.

Reed's hand slid behind his neck. A gesture she'd seen him do whenever his thoughts were heavy on his mind. In that way, he and Pat had been very much alike. She could read the two men as if they had indeed been blood brothers. "I don't suppose you and the girls would like to bunk at my house while we sort out this…" His gaze wandered to what was left of her home, but no more words came out.

And just like the furnace, and the windows, and the array of little things Reed continuously tried to help with, she knew she couldn't say yes. But what was she supposed to do?

"I'm guessing that stubborn glint in your eye means no?"

Blowing out a heavy sigh, she nodded. Maybe she could afford a few days at Meg's B&B while she checked on her insurance.

"You should probably know, the Ladies Afternoon Social Club are arguing over who is taking you in." His arm still hanging from his neck, the words brought a small smile to Reed's face. The first she'd seen from anyone all morning.

"That won't be necessary."

The hint of humor lifted to a full-blown grin. "I sure hope you don't expect me to tell them that?"

She knew he was right. The social club put an entirely new spin on southern hospitality. They'd all gone out of their way to make her and Pat feel welcome when they'd adopted Tuckers Bluff as their home, and again almost three years ago when a burst aneurism unexpectedly ripped the man, who had survived multiple tours of duty in the middle east, from her life. Of late they'd understood her need for peace and solitude; Pat had been the natural extrovert in the family, not her. Somewhere along the road, Eileen Farraday had spread the word that including Chloe in absolutely everything the town pulled together, stressed her last social nerve. It hadn't been so hard when she had Pat. He'd held her hand and kept her at ease, but on her own, she was happier, safer.

"And it looks like the winner is on her way." Reed stepped to one side, his grin still wide across his face.

She almost wished it had been anyone but Eileen. When they'd first moved to Tuckers Bluff, she'd been warned the family matriarch was a force to be reckoned with when she set her mind to something, and as sure as Chloe knew her own name, she knew she and the girls would be staying at the Farraday ranch.

"I'm afraid anything fabric in the girls' room is unsalvageable." Eileen managed to hold a smile through the less than pleasant news. "Catherine has some things of Stacey's that she's going to drop by and Allison is bringing by a few things of Brittany's for Sarah. That should keep us going till we have time to organize."

"Thank you." There was no point in arguing. She couldn't keep her girls in their pajamas while she sorted through the situation. "That's very kind of everyone."

"Sisters said as soon as you're up to it you and the girls can go shopping on them."

"That won't be necessary." Not that she knew how she was going to replace an entire hand me down wardrobe.

"No, it's not. But it's what we folks do. We take care of our own. And like it or not, you're one of us now."

For the first time in a very long while, she actually felt her heart lift. Being alone wasn't always everything it was cracked up to be.

• • • •

"They'll come through this just fine." DJ Farraday leaned on the back porch railing at his family's home.

Reed wasn't sure if his friend and supervisor was reassuring Reed or himself, but Reed appreciated the words nonetheless. As much as he would have preferred having Chloe and the girls under his own roof, he wasn't an idiot. The good people of Tuckers Bluff truly were good people, but gossip was gossip no matter where you went, and a single man and a widow with two small children were all the ingredients necessary for a doozy of a story.

Sean Farraday joined his son and Reed, handing each a longneck beer. "Thought you could use this."

"Thanks," the two muttered.

Waiting a beat for someone else to speak, Reed took in a long swallow and finally asked, "How's it going inside?"

"As well as could be expected. Everyone's treating supper like any other Sunday. Emmie is playing with Stacey and Sarah is coloring with Allison and Brittany. The rest of the clan are either peeling potatoes or setting the table or finding some other busy work."

"We should probably get inside and do our share." Reed pushed back from the railing.

Sean Farraday shook his head. "We did more than our share today. The others want to help too."

Even though Reed knew his words were spot on, it didn't stop him from wanting to go inside and do something, anything, at least see for himself how Chloe was holding up.

"You two know that Pat would be damn glad he moved his family here." Once again Sean gave voice to the thoughts no one was saying.

Neither he nor DJ could manage a nod. Aneurisms were the kind of thing that killed people in big cities just the same as in small counties, but second guessing if Pat could have been saved if he and his family had chosen to settle in Dallas or Houston was something Reed had become accustomed to.

Raising one brow, Sean took a slow swallow, shifting his gaze from DJ to Reed and back. "Don't you two go beating up on yourselves. We may not have saved the house but we saved Pat's family and that's all that matters."

This time, like matching bookends, he and DJ bobbed their heads. Everyone was alive and well. That was indeed all that mattered. Now the next question hanging over everyone's head had to be asked. "Where do we start?"

There wasn't any doubt that this would be a town effort. That's just the way Tuckers Bluff operated. Reed was pretty sure Chloe had some insurance, but bureaucracies of any kind never ran well. With Christmas only a few weeks away, he already knew his goal. Get Chloe and the girls settled as soon as possible.

"If I know my wife." Sean paused a moment to grin at his own words. He and Eileen were still in the newlywed stage. "She's already lining up the work schedule."

The porch door squeaked open and a three foot tall bundle with bright blue eyes and golden locks came shuffling up to Reed and latched onto his leg.

Without hesitating, he bent over and scooted her up into his arms. "How's it going, sweet pea?"

Sarah leaned her head against his shoulder but didn't say a word. The more reserved of the two girls, Sarah had always stuck close to her mom. Emmie had been more of a daddy's girl, which made him occasionally wonder if Pat had been around after Sarah was born, would she have followed suit. Today she'd spent most of the afternoon attached to Reed's leg or perched in his arms. It had taken quite a bit of coaxing by Allison to get her to stay in the family room and color with the other children. Apparently the novelty had worn off quickly.

"Looks like you've got a new friend." Sean smiled.

Reed nodded. He wasn't sure what to make of the sudden attachment. Perhaps because he'd been the first one to reach her hiding place from the fire, or maybe he happened to be the adult male in the crowd she was the most used to seeing. Whichever the answer, he was glad to be here for her.

"There you are." Chloe stepped onto the porch and to Reed's surprise, despite Chloe's outstretched arms, Sarah made no effort to reach for her mother. "We can't impose on Uncle Reed, sweetie."

Sarah's delicate little arms tightened around his neck.

"I don't mind." Gently he stroked her back and a sense of contentment settled inside him when the sweet little girl eased her grip and relaxed into his shoulder again.

"I know, but—"

"Really. It's fine." Reassuring a frightened little girl was the least he could do to make a difficult day a little easier. He'd done it too many times for strangers. It was the least he could do for Pat's family.

"Miss Toni made a chocolate cake especially for us," Chloe coaxed.

Reed would have thought that chocolate cake would be enough to entice any little girl, but Sarah simply shook her head.

"How about we both go inside and sample some of that cake?" he asked

The little cherub bobbed her head against him.

"Looks like we're all going inside for some cake." Reed smiled. After all, what adult male wanted to say no to Toni's cake. He wasn't sure why Brooks wasn't the size of an elephant. With a wife who baked like Toni, the man had to be on constant sugar overload.

The hum of activity enveloped him as soon as he crossed the threshold. Sunday supper at the Farraday house reminded him of any retro TV show of the good old days. Lots of family, lots of love, and always plenty of food. And cake.

"Perfect timing," Aunt Eileen called from the kitchen sink. "Connor just took the roast to the dining room."

"One of you take this." Adam's wife Meg stretched out her arms holding a large bowl of mashed potatoes.

"I need another tomato." Allison dropped a handful of chopped veggies into a large salad bowl. Living next door, Connor's wife was as much at home in the Farraday kitchen as Aunt Eileen.

"Here." Becky popped her head out of the fridge, paused to give her husband DJ a small peck on the cheek, then cradling multiple bottles of dressing in her arms, handed a tomato off to Catherine.

"Thanks!" Catherine smiled, dicing with the precision that had come from years of helping prep large family dinners.

Even after the bone-weary day, the interaction made him smile. Not so with little Sarah or her mom. Chloe seemed more lost and alone than ever, even in the middle of the dining room full of people, and Sarah wouldn't let go of her death grip around his neck. Today's fire might prove to be the only thing on the planet that a little Farraday comfort couldn't fix.

CHAPTER THREE

"It's very kind of you to open your home to us." Chloe had practiced these words in her head most of the night. All through the massive family dinner, the monumental effort at a normal bedtime routine in a strange home with strange belongings and near strangers, and now in the blissful peace of a near empty kitchen and a cup of warm tea, she found the chance to speak. "We really do appreciate it."

"I wish we could do more." Eileen extended her hand and enfolded the back of Chloe's clenched fist in her warmth. "You can rest assured we'll have you home again very soon."

One hand resting on his wife's shoulder, Sean Farraday nodded and took a sip of his hot cocoa.

She'd had such high hopes for this Christmas. The last couple of years Chloe had done her best to keep up her spirits for the girls, but Christmas without Pat just wasn't the same. This year she'd decided they were going to go all out the way they used to. She'd even decided to ask Reed to help her hang the lights outside and maybe join them for the annual Main Street Parade. Now, with the fire, she didn't have a clue how she was going to pull off a real Christmas. Out in the middle of west Texas with little interruption from the insanity of the modern world was a great place to raise children, but not so great for insurance adjusters to reach. She'd been making mental lists for hours. As folks chatted around the table about food, and school, and horses, and a myriad of other things she'd already forgotten, her mind went room by room, making note of what had to be replaced now and what could wait. The sheer length of the ever-growing list with no room for anything even closely related to a Merry Christmas was almost enough to send her running to hide under the nearest covers and not come up for air until her daughters graduated college.

"Now." Eileen straightened in her seat and pulled a bundle from a nearby basket. "I had started these Christmas stockings earlier in the year for the Christmas bazaar and never got them finished." Unraveling a strand of needlepoint thread, she smiled at Chloe. "I thought Sarah might like the one with the snowman and Emmie the one with Santa."

Overcome by the thoughtfulness, Chloe bit her lower lip and shook her head.

"No?" Eileen asked. "You're right. Sarah is smaller she'll appreciate the Santa one better." Pencil in hand, Eileen proceeded to trace the girls name on the white band.

"I'm sorry. What I meant was that I'm sure the girls will like anything you do for them. This is so very nice of you."

The needle threaded, Eileen continued to smile and slowly stabbed at the stocking, tracing the penciled name. "I just needed a good excuse to finish them. Tell me what else can we do to make you and the girls feel more at home here?"

"Oh, you've already done too much."

Eileen shook her head. "We have barely begun. Our work is cut out for us. Especially with the holidays around the corner. Christmas is always so special with children."

As far as Chloe was concerned, everything about Christmas should be special for everyone. She'd always loved this time of year. But Eileen had a point, it was considerably more fun stringing popcorn and making ornaments with the girls. She and Pat had always enjoyed starting little holiday traditions, but once Emmie was born she elevated the fun to an all new level.

The back door slammed and Finn Farraday tromped inside, cleaning his boot heels before stepping into the kitchen. That was one thing Chloe had noticed earlier this evening. Eileen had trained all her clan well. Not a slacker in the bunch.

"Just left Sam at his cabin and we've pretty much got the schedule shifted around so you and I can walk the house tomorrow. Jamison has his buddy from Butler Springs meeting us.

If we're lucky most of the main structure will be salvageable."

Main structure? Salvageable? "Are we talking about my house?" she asked softly.

Finn and Sean nodded.

"The way I look at it," Finn pulled a pencil from behind his ear, a notepad from his pocket, and swung his leg over a kitchen chair, "if we don't find any surprises tomorrow, and if we can gather enough volunteers, we can start right away with the demo to get a head start and just maybe knock the whole thing out in time for Chloe and the girls to move home before Christmas."

Sean whistled sharply. "That's a tall order. The back half of the place is pretty much gone. We'll definitely be doing that section from the first floor up."

The entire conversation seemed totally surreal to Chloe. These men—neighbors, friends—were talking about her house as if it were their problem not hers.

"Makes sense to me. What do you say?" Sean looked to Chloe

It took a few seconds to realize she'd missed something key as the other three people in the room were staring at her. "I beg your pardon?"

"As long as we have to start from scratch, now would be a good time to make any upgrades, changes you've been wanting."

Her mind couldn't seem to process. "I, uh, don't know that the insurance will cover any upgrades." Hell, she wasn't even sure the insurance would cover making the house habitable again. Did these companies total houses the way they did cars? Would they require her to just tear it all down and start over again? Would there be enough money if they did?

"Your policy will probably cover current code and considering how old the place was, in the end you'll have a much safer house."

She knew in her mind somewhere that Sean was trying to reassure her, but it wasn't working.

"This," Eileen patted her hand again, "is going to be a living example for Sunday school and turning lemons into lemonade. The house will be darling when it's all done."

When it's all done. She was far from being a pessimist, but Chloe had the feeling that the Farradays had been drinking a little too much of the kids' Kool-Aid. Nothing in life was as easy as they were making it sound. She'd learned that lesson the hard way.

While Sean and his son bantered back and forth about electricians and the all-around general shortage of tradesmen in Tuckers Bluff, the casual use of the word Christmas kept flying up at her. Her gaze fell on a traditional paper calendar hanging by the back door, one from the hardware store Grace's husband Chase owned. Christmas really was right around the corner. The Farradays weren't only optimists if they thought all in her world could be right again by the holidays, they'd each lost their ever-loving minds. Even if Santa and all his little elves descended on Tuckers Bluff and did the work themselves, no way would her life be back in order for the Christmas holiday. Not without a miracle.

• • • •

Leaving Chloe and the girls at the Farraday's had been harder than Reed expected, but his shift was coming up too soon and he needed sleep. Not that he believed he'd get any rest. Even if Chloe was in the best of hands, he still couldn't get away from the memory of the dazed expression that had remained on her face all day.

Sinking onto the bed, he leaned over to pull off his boots. One then the other landed on the hardwood floor with a thud. Slowly lifting his head, he let his gaze scan the room. Six months and he had more boxes than furniture in the master. Heck, his whole house looked like the moving truck had just pulled away from the front door. How was he supposed to help get Chloe's house back together when his own home still looked like he hadn't quite moved in?

It took a few long minutes to lift himself off the bed. He'd cleaned up some after fighting the fire, before landing at the

Farraday's for supper, but now every muscle in his body screamed for a very long, very hot shower. With each step his mind repainted a picture from earlier in the day. Kicking his jeans into the laundry basket, he reached into the shower and adjusted the water temperature. A picture of Pat handing out cigars the day Emmie was born flashed through his mind. It had been such a happy day. He undid the last button on his shirt and bundling it into a ball, hurled it across the small bath like a three-point court shot. Ignoring the images of a once happy family continuing to play in his mind, he muttered "score" as the wadded shirt swirled around the inside of the hamper rim.

The best part of a hot shower had to be the steam-filled air. The pulsing water on his back came close, but the steam seeped into every pore and went a long way toward making him feel human again. Yet nothing wiped away the memory of the look on Chloe's face or the feel of little Sarah clinging to him most of the day.

His cell phone sounded from the bedroom and turning the shower off with one hand and reaching for a towel with the other, he bolted across the room and snagged the phone from the nightstand. "Hello."

"How you holding up?" DJ's voice came through the line.

"Fine."

"Keegan is offering to take your shift tonight."

Reed ran his hand across the back of his neck. Assuming he could fall asleep, a good night's rest would make helping Chloe tomorrow easier. After all, he wouldn't be much good to anyone falling asleep on his feet. "That would be great."

"Listen," DJ paused, "I know you're as worried as the rest of us, but try and get some sleep. Things will probably get harder before they get easier. She's been through more than her share."

"Yeah." Didn't he know that. As stunned as Chloe was today, he suspected tomorrow was going to descend with a boom. "Tell Keegan I said thanks."

"Will do. See you tomorrow."

Reed disconnected and stared at his phone. Despite the fire and water damage to the house, Chloe's phone survived safely tucked away in her handbag. The temptation to call and check up on her tugged at him. His gaze flickered to the nearby clock. It wasn't very late. Most likely she was still awake. *Maybe.* Exhaustion might have taken over. Or she might be consoling the girls. Or he could just text and hope he didn't disturb her if she was resting.

Do you have everything you need? He stared at the phone.

Yes. Thank you. Eileen and Sean are wonderful. She made the girls their own stockings and hung them on the mantel with the rest of the family.

That was nice of her.

A moment later, his phone buzzed. Chloe.

"Hello."

"The girls fell asleep. Emmie asked for an extra story but she was out like a light halfway through."

The sound of her voice soothed the tension already building between his shoulders. "That's good. This had to be so frightening for them."

"I think they're torn between the moments of fear and the fun adventure after their hero showed up."

"I don't know about that."

"I do. The way Emmie chattered on about you, I'm pretty sure you rode up on your white horse seconds before appearing in her room and whisking her out to safety."

"Connor carried her out."

"But you got to her first. No matter how you look at it you're the knight in shining armor."

"I suppose I've been called worse things."

Chloe chuckled.

The sound made him smile. Slowly he eased onto the bed again. He didn't know what to say. "If you need anything, no matter what time, just call."

"I doubt I'll need anything. Eileen is taking care of things before I have time to think of them."

This time he chuckled. He'd been on the receiving end of Aunt Eileen's generosity more than once.

"Do you really think we'll be able to be home for Christmas?" Her voice came out low and soft and reminded him of her daughters.

He had no idea how to pull it off. Chloe had done such a great job decorating the tree. He'd wished he could have been there to help string the cranberries and popcorn garland, but the least he could do now was give it his all to give them back their Christmas in their own home. Besides, the faster the girls were back to their normal, the less of a negative impact this entire ordeal would have on them. "That's the plan."

"Are you coming with us to see the house tomorrow?"

"Absolutely. Already confirmed with Sean and Finn. Want me to pick you up?"

"I'm sure I can hitch a ride with someone from the ranch."

"Let me know if things change."

"I will." The line went quiet for a few long moments. "I guess I should get some sleep."

He nodded before realizing she couldn't see him. "Sleep well, and remember—"

"Anything at all and I'll call you." He could hear the smile in her voice.

"Good night."

"Night. And Reed..."

"Yes."

"Thank you. For everything."

The call disconnected but he continued to stare at his screen. The next few weeks were going to be long and busy. DJ was more right than he knew. Things were very likely going to get harder and for reasons that had nothing to do with rebuilding a house.

CHAPTER FOUR

"I'll see your two and raise you two." Eileen tossed a couple of chips into the pot.

"Who's two?" Ruth, her friend of decades, frowned. "You raised my bet last round. It's time to show us what you've got."

"Oh." She glanced down at the cards displayed on the table and the ones she still held in her hands. She might be sitting at the Tuckers Bluff Ladies Afternoon Social Club's regular table, but her heart and thoughts were with those in her family over at Chloe's. Wondering how it's going. Debating in her mind how much work would they have to do.

"Well?" Dorothy asked.

Eileen set her cards down. "I guess I'm a little distracted."

"A little?" Ruth shook her head and gathered the cards.

"Okay," Eileen nudged her cards in Ruth's direction, "a lot. My heart goes out to Chloe and the girls." When she'd heard that the two dogs had alerted Reed to the fire, the hairs on the back of her neck stood on end at the thought of how long it might have taken anyone else to notice the smoke. Even now the possibilities of what would have happened to that family if the rescuers had delayed even another ten minutes made her heart skip a beat.

Dorothy tossed a chip into the pot for the next hand. "We all feel the same way."

Ruth nodded. "Whole town feels that way."

"And as soon as Sean and the others report back, we'll all know where to start," Sally May added.

Eileen was probably more worried about Chloe's spirit than her house. It hadn't taken long after Pat's death for Eileen and the others to figure out that while Chloe was as nice as they came, she also didn't handle crowds well. And as far as Eileen could tell, anything more than two people in a room constituted a crowd for Chloe.

"More tea?" Abby stood over Eileen's shoulder, a pitcher of tea in hand.

All four women shook their heads. To their surprise, rather than a few brief words or moving on to the folks at the next table, Abby pulled up a chair and took a seat.

"You're playing cards with us?" Sally May asked.

"Of course not. I just wanted to find out what's the deal with Chloe. Jamie and I want to help."

"We all do," Ruth said.

"I know. We were talking early this morning and if Chloe likes antiques, she's welcome to her pick of what's in the attic at the pub."

"Good." Eileen patted her niece-in-law's hand. "That's a great place to start. She pretty much lost everything inside. If it wasn't burned, it was smoked, or drowned."

"They're going to need just about everything and insurance always takes forever to come through." Ruth shuffled the cards in front of her and sighed. "This whole mess is going to require more than some frozen casseroles or welcome baskets."

Dorothy nodded. "Even Toni's cake balls won't make this much better."

Somewhere between the crack of dawn and cranking the engine on her old suburban to come to town, Eileen had stopped dwelling on just how much work was ahead of them, no matter how much damage, and pondered the dogs. Under normal circumstances what lie ahead could be daunting, but she'd learned whenever the dogs were involved things seemed to just, well, work out. Still, there was so very much to be worked out. A little family was at stake. Fortunately, somewhere between sunrise and Main Street, she'd gotten an idea. A darn good one—but she'd have to work fast.

• • • •

Despite how badly Chloe had wanted keep both her girls with her today, Aunt Eileen had suggested last night, and again this morning over coffee, that rather than keeping Emmie home, the routine of school and friends was best for her little girl. Shortly after an early breakfast, Allison volunteered to have Sarah play with Britney rather than be subjected to viewing what was left of their home. Both women had been very convincing. Not that it had taken much convincing, Chloe had fretted most of the night over how to handle this morning. She'd even considered not joining everyone for the walk through. Now standing in front of the charred home, she almost wished she'd made a play date anywhere else for herself. The front hadn't been too bad. For a few moments she let herself believe that the entire incident had been nothing more than a very bad dream.

Then they'd walked into the house. The once creamy living room walls, what were left of them, now sported a sickening shade of charcoal black. Letting her gaze carry to the back of the room, past the shadow of what was once their Christmas tree, through the burned studs with a clear view of her backyard, the air briefly stuck in her throat.

"Are you okay?" Reed's soothing low voice reached her moments before his hand rested on the small of her back.

She nodded. If she repeated she was fine often enough, maybe she would be. "My house," she mumbled. She didn't even want to consider that this mess was directly under her daughters' room.

Sean Farraday and his sons were already deep in conversation in what was left of the kitchen with a man Chloe didn't recognize. Most likely the architect friend mentioned after dinner last night. Or was it engineer? Did it matter?

Walking past the charred tree, she paused, looking over her shoulder. "Oh."

Only a half step behind her, Reed stopped as well.

From behind, the tree looked almost untouched. A bit soggy

from the dousing and a little singed on some of the tips, but overall, the ornaments hung almost smiling at her. Inching forward, she reached for two of her favorites. A lovely little pink rocking horse commemorating Emmie's first Christmas and brass star for Sarah's. "They made it."

"Some things never cease to surprise me." He reached for another one of her favorites. An old hand-painted bell in red, green and blue. It had belonged to her grandmother. One of the few treasures that reminded her of the woman who had raised her. Right about now a big hug and a slice of Nana's Dutch apple pie with fresh whipped cream would have gone a long way to making her day a little less painful.

"Oh, there you are." Sean Farraday patted the architect on the shoulder and moved to meet Chloe by the tree. "Pretty amazing how it survived."

Considering that everything else was toast, amazing was an understatement. "Yes. Very."

"We've established despite how awful things look, like the backside of the tree," Sean gestured, "most of the structural supports are in pretty good shape." He pointed overhead. "A few of these joists are a little too charred for comfort so we'll have to replace them, but that's it structurally."

She dared work her way through the kitchen to her room.

"It's pretty soggy. I doubt you'll want to save any of the clothing. It's best to rip out all the sheetrock and insulation to expose the studs. Make sure they're all sound, which they probably are, and dried out. Free of mold."

Chloe's limbs felt super heavy. Like her soles were made of cement, not rubber. Not till today did she realize a wet house had a smell all its own. Her fingers ran over the vanity that had once belonged to her grandmother. No way would she find a dry towel in the house and she desperately wanted to wipe all the water away. "I should come back with some towels. Do you have any fans?" She wasn't sure who she was asking. Deep down she knew a towel and a fan wouldn't be enough to salvage her treasures, but those were the only words that her mouth could form.

Reed settled his hand on her back again. "I have some rags in the car. I'll run and get them. We can put this out in the sun while we look around the rest of the house."

Never had she been so grateful to another human being for keeping rags in their car. The idea of doing something—anything—was almost enough to make her smile. Almost.

● ● ● ●

Reed raced out the door, down the front steps, and across to his car as if everyone's lives depended on his retrieving a few dry rags. Opening the trunk, he grabbed the plastic bag and spun on his heel. By the time he'd reached the front steps, Sean and Finn were carrying the old piece of furniture onto the porch.

"It's a cold day, but a little bit of sunshine might help," Sean told Chloe. The sadness lingering in her eyes tugged at every protective instinct he had, and judging by the looks on the other men's faces, theirs too.

For the next few hours they picked through the house. Pulling the few things out to the porch that with a little fresh air and wiping down might be salvaged, but truth be told, there wasn't much. The water needed to save the house had pretty much ruined everything inside. Not a single fabric item was worth salvaging and most of the furnishings were shot as well.

"Oh, look." A hint of a smile tugged at Chloe's face.

He had no idea what she'd found at the bottom of a closet, but he was thankful for anything that might bring a smile to her face.

"They're dry." She held out an old quilt. "Nana made these. I've been saving them till the girls were a little older to use on their beds."

"It's lovely." He wasn't exactly an expert on quilts, but the color combination was pleasing and the way her fingers gently glided across the top, he suspected the sentimental value to Chloe was worth a small fortune. His gaze drifted to the large plastic bag on the floor beside her and the second bag with another similar coverlet inside.

"I keep them in a zippered bag to protect them from dust. I guess in the middle of the closet and in the bags they were protected from the water too." Chloe shook her head and sighed. "I've been telling myself for so long that I should take them out and use them. Display them. Enjoy them. Now I'm so glad I didn't."

All he could offer was a smile and share the gratitude at one other item salvaged from the mess. Carefully, they cleaned and wrapped each rescued ornament in the pages of an old magazine from someone's truck. The sad thing was there had been so little to be salvaged that it had only taken a few hours to sort and pack. Sean and Finn had gone back to the ranch a bit ago. The plan was to get numbers and data all lined up so the insurance company could move faster.

"Last one." She smiled at him, carefully handing off the box of bundled ornaments. "I'm so glad you thought to bring some empty boxes."

"Me too." It was probably the only good idea he'd had all night. Though he didn't tell her how many more boxes were folded in his trunk in hopes that there would have been more to keep. Even though he'd seen enough devastation in his career to know better, he'd still hoped.

"Now the question is what to do with them?"

"I'll store them," Reed offered.

"I don't want to impose."

"It's not imposing. As a matter of fact, they'll fit right in with my current décor."

"What?" Her hands landed on her hips as she stepped back. "You're still not unpacked?"

"Not completely."

"Reed." Her toe started tapping. "You moved from a one bedroom apartment. How much unpacking could you have to do?"

He shrugged.

"All right." She shook her head. "Is your kitchen still in boxes?"

"No. It was a small kitchen."

Still shaking her head, she chuckled. "Do you still like lasagna?"

He nodded.

"I froze one last week. It's probably not very frozen any more. What do you say we have that for lunch and maybe I can repay a little of your time and help you unpack some of your stuff?"

"You don't have to do that."

"No. I don't." Her expression softened. "But I'd like to."

"Thanks."

"No. Thank *you*. For everything." Her hand landed on his arm and for a fast minute his mind went back to the first night they'd met. He'd nearly swallowed his tongue then too. She was smart, funny, and beautiful. And the minute she laid eyes on his buddy the two of them looked like they'd been struck upside the head with a two by four. In an instant Reed knew he'd lost a great gal to his best friend.

Maybe a cozy lunch wasn't the best idea he'd ever agreed to.

CHAPTER FIVE

The last thing Chloe had expected when Reed offered to store her stuff was that she would have an entire room for just her meager belongings. They stacked the few boxes neatly in one corner, loaded her freezer items into his, stuck the lasagna in the oven to warm, and now she was getting the two dollar tour. "Tell me again why this is the first time I'm seeing this place?"

Reed raised his brows, hefted one shoulder and holding back a smile, tipped his head. The gesture only added to that lost little boy look that had caught her eye so many years ago. She'd enjoyed talking with him until Pat emerged from a marathon pool game and swept her off her feet. Literally. Well. Maybe it was more knocked her off her feet. To this day she wasn't sure what he'd tripped on, but he'd stumbled across his buddy, sending himself and her tumbling over each other and onto the floor laughing so hard she almost peed her pants. It had been love at first bumble.

"I'm sorry the girls and I haven't come by sooner. Brought you a casserole or something. I'm afraid it was very un-neighborly of me."

"Don't think twice about it. I still haven't gotten through all the food the town brought over."

"That would explain why a bachelor has a nearly full freezer."

"It would."

One hand on her hip, she looked around the living room then pointed to a stack of boxes in one corner. "What's in those boxes over there?"

He hitched that cute lazy shoulder again. "Christmas stuff."

"Stuff?"

"The big one on the bottom is the tree, the little ones on top are things."

"Things?"

"You know. Decorations, ornaments. That sort of *thing*."

Her gaze scanned the room once more. It was sparsely decorated. She wasn't even sure the one print of Joe DiMaggio, Babe Ruth and Lou Gehrig counted as decoration and yet he had boxes of Christmas décor.

"My mom gave them to me."

What was he a mind reader now?

"Her house was a winter wonderland. Every year like clockwork, the day after Halloween, she started decorating. The lights and candles were all turned on the day after Thanksgiving and stayed up till just before Valentines Day."

Chloe nodded, waiting for more.

"When Mom and Dad moved to Florida they took what they needed for the condo and divvied the rest up between me and my siblings."

Now it all made sense. Except for the pained look on his face. "Bad memories?"

"What?" His face pinched in confusion.

"Halloween and Thanksgiving are over and you haven't taken the tape off the boxes."

"Oh. No. I love Christmas. I just feel like I should have unpacked regular household items by now. You know, before I start on the tree and all the garland and, well, *stuff*. I'm just glad Mom isn't here to see how bare this place looks."

"Okay." She clapped her hands together.

"Okay?"

"You heard me. The lasagna has a minimum of thirty minutes to go. In that time we can knock out at least a couple of boxes. Where do we start?"

"Start?"

"Have you always been this dense?"

"What?" Surprise rounded his eyes.

"Never mind." *Men*. She'd known Reed a lot of years. He was best man at their wedding. Deployed with her husband when Emmie was born, he'd stayed up all night pouring coffee into Pat until they'd heard mom and baby girl were doing great. When she lost Pat, he'd been the one to hold her together when she thought she couldn't make it another hour. When Sarah was born, he'd paced the hall at the hospital until the doctor came out and announced all was well.

She should know better than to expect any man to speak in full sentences when out of his element, and clearly putting his own house in order was not his thing. Spinning around, she made an executive decision. There were three boxes in the hall. That was as good a place as any to start. "Come on. We're clearing the hall of the obstacle course. We don't need you waking up in the middle of the night and breaking your neck in the dark."

He fell in step beside her. "I don't think three boxes counts as an obstacle course."

"If you say so."

"I do."

"I'm not going to find anything weird, am I?"

"Weird?"

There he went again with those one word answers. "You know, like girlie magazines."

She didn't know which was cuter, the blush or the sputtered laugh. "No girlie magazines. I think they're mostly linens. Towels and sheets and things."

"I'm not even going to ask what you've been sleeping on."

"It's faster to wash and dry my sheets than unpack."

"On what planet?" She looked over her shoulder at him. "Never mind. Don't answer that."

Using his pocket knife, he slit the tape open on one box then the next two.

The first box was all towels. Instead of the mismatched bachelor towels leftover from college that she'd expected to find she uncovered matching bath sheets in complimentary shades of blue and gray. "They match."

"The blues were in my master, the gray for company. I suppose now they'll go in the hall bath."

Without looking at him, she began refolding the towels the way she liked them. She'd already done two when she noticed him folding to match her. "Is this all right?"

"You'd have made a great marine. Any sergeant would be pleased with your neat folding."

In only a few minutes, they'd folded all the towels and placed them neatly in the linen closet at the end of the hall. The sheets weren't quite as easy. He had a king sized bed. Though she had no idea what a single man needed with a bed big enough for a platoon.

Holding two edges in one hand, she gave him the other end. "Help with the corners, please."

She stood at one end of the long hall and made the first fold. Reed followed her lead. They met in the middle when it was time for the smaller folds. Next came the fitted sheets. Those took a little more calculating. Folded over her hand, she kept dropping her end and laughing. "Have you ever considered a smaller bed? The sheets are way easier to fold."

"We don't have to be this neat about it." He slid his fists into the two corners and walked up to her. "There won't be a linen closet inspection at end of day."

"It's the principle of the thing," she insisted, once again sliding the corners onto her hand and closing the gap between them. "All I have to do is slide my side over yours."

They bumped arms. She flipped her ends on top of his, her hands closing over his. Layers of fabric between them, she lifted her gaze to meet his. He stood perfectly still, his hands tucked under the layer of bedding. He didn't move back, didn't take possession. He just stared into her eyes. For the second time today, she found it hard to breathe.

It was time to step back, walk away, let him finish folding his sheet, but she couldn't drag her gaze away from his. "Almost finished."

"Yes." He nodded but didn't move.

Neither did she. She didn't want to. Didn't want to take her hands away. Didn't want to break the connection. And she didn't understand why, but standing in the middle of the hall, sharing a semi-folded king size sheet between them, having someone to work beside her, she felt more at peace than she had in an awfully long time. And what the heck was she supposed to do about that?

• • • •

Didn't he probably look the idiot, standing in the hallway gaping at Chloe like a deer in the headlights. Forcing himself to step back, he slipped his hands out from under hers, crossed the final two corners into one, and finished folding the sheet. "I'll put this in the closet."

"Yes," she mumbled, stepping slowly back. "I think I'd better check the lasagna."

Nice going, Taylor. The woman was probably disoriented enough after yesterday and this morning. She didn't need him acting like an awkward teenager. Grabbing the remaining fitted sheet, he did a halfhearted fast fold and shoved it into the closet under the others. He hoped she didn't do an inspection, but he couldn't bring himself to come in that close contact with her again. Not today.

Grabbing the empty box, he broke it up, folding it flat and headed to the kitchen. "Wow, this smells amazing."

"It's a little cold on the inside. A few more minutes should do it."

"Sounds good." He walked over to the fridge. "Would you like something cold to drink?"

"Just water for me, thank you."

"Water it is." He grabbed a bottle for her, and a real sugar Mexican cola for himself.

"Ooh. I haven't had one of those in ages."

"It's not too late to change your mind." He loved the way she nibbled on her lower lip when contemplating something she really wanted to do. She'd done that for as long as he had known her.

"You only live once, right?"

He held back a chuckle. "I gather that's a yes?"

"Please."

"One real cola coming up." Using the old-fashioned opener screwed under one side of the sink, he popped the tops off.

Accepting the bottle he handed her, she followed him into the living room and flopped, one leg bent underneath her, into the big easy chair. Her head tipped slightly back, she took a long slow swallow. "Oh, that really hits the spot."

His mind went in a hundred different directions, none of which were even slightly appropriate under the circumstances. Instead of saying something stupid, he took a long swallow himself.

"Do you remember that time you decided to lay a brick patio in our backyard?" Rather than look at him, her gaze remained focused on the bottle in her hand.

He remembered that day well. The memory made him laugh. "I certainly do. What made you think of that now?"

"I guess it's the way you tipped that bottle up. Something about it reminded me of that day. Except then you guys were drinking Coronas, not colas."

"As I remember, it was a very hot day."

"It was." She nodded. "But somehow I lost count of how much you guys had drunk before you finished my patio."

"It was a good, solid patio."

She shook her head. "It may have been solid, but it wasn't exactly square. Narrow on one side, widening to the other, had the bricks been yellow instead of red it would've reminded me of the Wizard of Oz and the yellow brick road."

It might have been a little off kilter. "It wasn't that bad. Besides, we fixed it, didn't we?"

"You did. And it's beautiful." She tipped her bottle at him. "Just goes to show how differently things turn out when you wait until you're finished to break out the beer."

"Duly noted."

A nostalgic glint lingered in her eye. Leaning forward, she set the bottle on the table. "You're a good looking guy. Why hasn't some nice girl reeled you in?"

How was he supposed to answer that one? "I guess I just don't have a lot of time to socialize."

Frowning, she leaned back in her chair. Taking one more sip, she tipped her head left then right, squeezing her eyes before rolling her neck.

He probably should've stayed exactly where he was, a safe distance away on the sofa, but he couldn't ignore the slight grimace as she turned her head back and forth. Walking around behind her, he gently placed his fingers along the curve of her neck and immediately found that tight spots that no amount of twisting or turning was going to relieve.

"Oh, that feels really nice." Her head lolled forward and she almost purred. "Really nice."

"You've got some really tight muscles."

"It's been a rough couple of days."

That it had.

One eye open, she craned her neck to briefly look at him over her shoulder. "Have you ever been in love?"

In love? How the heck had they gone from the yellow brick road to his love life? It took a few seconds to form a reasonable yet honest answer. "Not really."

Her head relaxed again from his ministrations, she rested her chin against her chest. "What's the difference between no and not really?"

When had he lost control of this conversation? "I guess once there was a girl I could have fallen in love with."

"Could have? What happened?"

"She married somebody else."

CHAPTER SIX

In the days that had passed since the fire, Chloe had come to realize there was definitely safety in numbers. When Pat had died unexpectedly, the town had done its best to rally around her, and she had done her best to push them away. There had been a minor tug and pull until they'd found their peace with each other. This time it was clear there would be no tugging or pulling. The Farradays were in her problems up to their elbows and nothing she did or said was going to change that. And for the first time in ages she was glad for the help.

Giggles carried easily into the kitchen from the family room. In less than a week, Stacey and Emmie had become thick as proverbial thieves. They rode to school together, did homework together, hung out in the barns together and tonight her older daughter would be spending her first sleepover at Stacey's.

One week ago, she knew of Stacey Farraday, Connor and Catherine Farraday's daughter. She'd seen the little girl in Emmie's class at least a few times, but hadn't truly had a chance to get to know her. What a difference a few days make.

"Rehab on your house starts first thing Monday morning." Sean Farraday poured himself a glass of milk.

While the prospect of having her house put back together should have been reason enough to make Chloe dance a jig, she hadn't gotten any numbers from the insurance company yet. "I don't understand."

"It pays to have friends in high places," Eileen teased, leaning against her husband and planting a small kiss on his cheek. "Or at least friends with lots more friends."

Despite her nature to keep to herself and her girls, she'd already grown very fond of the Farradays. The banter, the jokes, but mostly the sincere affection that bounced around the rooms like a living thing. What she hadn't figured out was how to interpret some of the inside jokes or what often appeared as good old-fashioned mind reading. Especially between Eileen and Sean.

Still she had no idea what Sean was talking about.

"What my wife means," Sean paused long enough to wink at his wife, "is that several key suppliers have agreed to allow us to get started now and pay when the insurance settlement comes in. The dumpster should be delivered some time tomorrow so that we can start chucking what can't be restored."

"Unkie!" Sarah's excited cry interrupted the conversation. As much as Sarah loved to chatter, she had yet to master the words "Uncle Reed." For as long as she could talk, Reed had always been just *Unkie* to Sarah.

Silence reigned in the kitchen until, grinning toddler in arm, Reed crossed the threshold into the kitchen. "Evening."

"Honey, you can't hang on to Uncle Reed all the time."

The second the words were out of Chloe's mouth, her daughter's hold tightened around Reed's neck. Her body language screamed, *oh yes I can, watch me*.

Gently, Reed patted young Sarah's shoulder. "I understand the big girls are getting ready to go out to the barn and help their uncle Adam with the new foal."

Whether it was the prospect of being considered one of the big girls or getting to visit the baby horse in the barn, Chloe had no idea, but her daughter forgot her strangling grip on Reed and sprouted a delighted smile.

"You come," Sarah muttered softly

Reed's gentle gaze met Chloe's, and she easily saw his silent request to let him cater to her little girl. Most likely there wasn't a woman on the planet who could resist his charm, and she doubted any mother would begrudge her daughter a chance to spend more time with such a thoughtful man and of course, the newborn horse.

"If Uncle Reed doesn't mind, it's fine with me." Besides she didn't like the idea of the children alone in the barn while Adam worked. All the Faraday men were responsible and careful with the next generation, but distractions happened and she just felt better knowing another adult would be in there.

"Care to join us, Mom?" Reed asked.

"Yes," Eileen added. "You really should see the foal."

"Oh." She looked to Sean. "I suppose we can finish this conversation in a bit?"

"Conversation?" Reed looked from one person to the next.

Sean nodded. "I was just telling Chloe that we've arranged for a dumpster delivery to start demo Monday morning. And of course Chase at the hardware store has agreed to postpone payment of supplies until the insurance company settles."

Chloe was torn between shaking her head, stomping her feet, and declaring absolutely not. Under no circumstances was she allowing any work to be done on her home before she knew exactly how much insurance money she had available. On the other hand, as much as she was enjoying her time with the Farradays, the idea of settling back into her own home sooner than later to celebrate Christmas just her and her girls was more than appealing. Or was it? Once again, she scanned the kitchen, seeing the joyful anticipation on her young daughter's face. Taking in all the faces of the people merrily moving about, somehow making sense of the chaos. The people who had taken her in like family. And even now as they spoke, were making plans to get her home put back together, better than before. Maybe a little extra chaos at Christmas wasn't such a bad thing after all?

"Why don't y'all run along with the girls." Sean pointed at the back door with his chin. "Nothing has to be decided right this minute."

Five minutes later, with Sarah still clinging to Reed, and like ducklings after their mother, the troop followed Adam down the path to the barn.

She leaned closer to Reed's side. "I thought baby animals were born in the spring?"

Reed nodded. "That's right. But the Farradays have two

seasons for calves and foals. Spring and now."

"Oh, I see."

As clingy as Sarah had been with Reed, the second she laid eyes on the little horse, she scrambled out of his arms and hurried to keep up with her older sister. Maybe some things would never change.

Reed chuckled. "So much for adoration."

"Try not to take it personally. I've been thrown over for much less than a pony."

"I'll keep that in mind."

Any bystander could see the Farradays loved Christmas. Actually, the entire town of Tuckers Bluff loved Christmas. Ever since Thanksgiving, Main Street had Christmas music playing from speakers hung all along the street. A live manger with real camels and donkeys that drew people from every neighboring town for weeks anchored one end of Main Street and the massive Christmas tree stood proud at the other end. Folks dressed in costume from the days of Charles Dickens strolled the street singing traditional carols, entertaining visitors and shoppers alike. One of her favorite events used to be the annual Christmas Eve parade of floats with bands and elves and snowmen followed by the expected Santa and his sleigh at the end. Of course, through all of this there were enough decorations and lights to outdo a Disney park, and the Farradays weren't far behind. It shouldn't have surprised her to discover even the inside of the barn was decked out in colorful lights. Garland and bows draped each stall door.

Adam had given the girls a detailed list of basic instructions while near the horses. Key on the list had been to watch where they walked. Chloe knew by the way Sarah followed the instructions and watched her every step that her baby was growing up. She wasn't sure she liked that one bit.

"Oh, Mommy look." Standing next to Adam and the young horse, Emmie pointed up.

Following her daughter's finger, it only took a second to spot the particular decoration.

"It's Mrs. Toe."

Chloe bit back a grin at her daughter's confusion.

"Aunt Eileen says whenever you stand underneath Mrs. Toe, you have to kiss whoever is next to you." Emmie flung her arms around the foal and planted a big kiss on its jaw line. Somehow, Chloe didn't think that's what Aunt Eileen had had in mind when she taught the girls about mistletoe, but this was definitely one of those photo ops that made her wish she hadn't left her phone in the house.

"Your turn, Mommy." Emmie pointed at Chloe.

At first she thought her daughter wanted her to hug the horse as well, but then she realized Emmie's attention was focused directly above her. Tipping her head back she spotted more mistletoe. A lot of it. Who the heck fills a barn with mistletoe? The stuff was all over the place. And the one her daughter pointed to hung directly over her and Reed.

When she dragged her gaze away from the offending sprig, her eyes met Reed's as his gaze slowly dropped from the mistletoe to her face. She didn't know who looked more panicked at the sudden revelation, her or him.

"You have to kiss, Mommy."

Yes, yes she did, because making a fuss would probably just draw more attention to exactly how nervous the idea of kissing Reed, even chastely under the mistletoe, made her.

Reed must have come to the same conclusion because a thin smile tipped one side of his mouth upward in an amused grin seconds before he dipped his chin and pressed a very short and very chaste kiss against her lips. She resisted the urge to touch her lips, took a step back and decided she was going to have to be more careful and pay a lot better attention to where all the sprigs were.

• • • •

In all these years, he'd hugged his best friend's wife more than a time or two. Once in a while he'd even given her a friendly peck on the cheek. The normal interactions that came with life in a friendly small town. Even so, somehow they had never found themselves standing under mistletoe, and if they had, a chaste meeting of lips with your buddy's wife wouldn't have been a big deal. So why did it feel like such a big deal today?

Because he was overthinking it. So what if the brief touch of her lips still had his tingling. He was overthinking everything lately. Like how did he go from a casual friend of the family that little Sarah never gave a second thought about, to having the sweet toddler sound asleep on his shoulder? He was sure it had something to do with the fear and the fire and his sudden appearance, but he hoped to hell none of it was going to cause permanent problems for her.

Sucking in a long, slow breath, his fingers gently raked Sarah's baby fine hair. If only he could go back and insist on replacing that blasted heater.

"Would you like some more coffee?" Speaking softly, Aunt Eileen stood smiling over him with a carafe in hand.

"That would be nice." He shifted his weight slightly, careful not to wake Sarah, then taking hold of the cup beside him, lifted it up.

"Black, right?"

He nodded.

Her back to the others in the room, she refilled his cup, then leaned in. "They're always so sweet when they're sleeping. You holding up okay?"

"She's not very heavy."

Aunt Eileen straightened. Staring at the sleeping child, she pressed her lips and barely shook her head. "You've been a real blessing to that family."

He probably should have done more. Since Pat's death he'd done what he could. Been as much of a friend as Chloe would allow, but he couldn't help think as much as he'd tried, he should have tried harder. "I don't know about that. You've done all the hard work. Opening your home to Chloe and the girls, making them feel like part of the family, fixing supper every night and including me—"

"Of course you'd be included," she almost snapped. "You're like family now."

The last couple of years as her own nephews had one by one married and moved out, and his mom and dad had relocated to Florida, Aunt Eileen had been especially good about including him in big family gatherings and the weekly Sunday suppers. Under normal circumstances he would never have imposed on them every night of the week, but he'd been considering the girls and Chloe and the aftershocks of the fire. When each day Aunt Eileen had stressed wanting him to join them for dinner, he didn't look a gift horse in the mouth. Though he couldn't do much, just seeing for himself they were mostly all right went a long way toward his peace of mind. Though he wouldn't feel totally at peace until everyone was in their own home and life was back to normal.

Not long ago, Chloe had left to take Emmie and Stacey back to Connor's for their sleepover. Sarah had refused to leave his side and somehow, before he knew what happened, she was sound asleep and Chloe was on her way next door. Not that he minded. Sarah had always been a mama's girl. Attached at Chloe's hip. But ever since the fire, she'd seemed fixated on him. How he hoped something as simple as getting them back in their own home was the answer to all his concerns.

From the nearby sofa, Sean Farraday grinned down at the sleeping toddler. "I'd swear it was only yesterday Grace was that age."

"They really do grow up fast." Finn came into the living room.

His father frowned at him. "How would you know?"

"Hey, we've all watched Brittany and Helen grow up. I'd swear it was just yesterday they were little babies that we were afraid to hold for fear we'd break them. Now they run almost as fast as I do."

"Slight exaggeration," Sean threw in.

"Not by much." Aunt Eileen re-entered the room, carrying her own mug of tea. "It's time for more babies in the house."

"Trying to tell me something?" Sean teased his wife.

Aunt Eileen's only response was to roll her eyes and mutter, "Men."

"She has a point." Finn sank into the empty arm chair.

"See." Aunt Eileen flashed a toothy grin and Reed bit back a smile. He loved this crazy family.

"Anyhow." Finn leaned forward. "I've been looking at the extended forecast. Unless we want the place waterlogged again, I think we need to start with the roof."

"I was thinking the same thing." Sean Farraday pushed to his feet and ran his hand across the back of his neck. "I've been giving it some thought. I think it's time to call Patrick."

"Maybe if he doesn't tell Aunt Mariah that he's coming to Tuckers Bluff, Uncle Patrick could make it work."

"I swear," Aunt Eileen huffed, "that woman sure knew how to make a mountain out of a molehill. It's been almost twenty years."

"Might as well have been yesterday." Sean tipped his head back before spinning around and facing his family. "But this is important. There's no way we can get a roofing crew here this time of year and I think it's important the little ones get back in their home in time for Christmas."

Two things crossed Reed's mind. First, that maybe with a little help from an internet video he could volunteer to help with the roof. And second, who the heck was Uncle Patrick?

CHAPTER SEVEN

"How's it going?" Ruth tossed a piece of sheet rock into a wheelbarrow. In order to speed up the prep work, anyone who could take the day off to help did. The Ladies Afternoon Social Club were in charge of the girls' room.

Yanking at another section of wall, Eileen shook her head. "Not so well. I figured after all this time it would be easier."

"Mistletoe didn't work?" Dorothy asked.

"Depends how you look at it. According to Emmie, they kissed in the barn. But I haven't been able to get them back to the barn since."

Sally May tossed a charred wood scrap onto the pile. "What about in the house?"

"Sean almost lost his eyeballs when he saw all the mistletoe we'd strung in the barn. No way he's letting me put even one sprig in the house."

Pulling on another section of sheet rock, Ruth tripped backward. "Maybe we should just let nature take its course. After all, it's worked fine for everyone else in the family."

"It's not nature's course I'm worried about, it's nature's timetable." As far as Eileen was concerned, the dog's appearance cemented what she herself had thought for over a year.

Dorothy took a step back and hefted her gloved hands on her hips. "Maybe they don't need tricks. What they need is time alone."

Squinting in thought, Ruth studied Dorothy. "You know, she has a point. Think about it. When does a single mother of two ever get much time alone?"

"Ain't that the truth," Dorothy concurred.

Sally May nodded her head. "She is right."

"Of course I'm right. So if Chloe never gets time to herself, how would Chloe and Reed get any time to themselves?"

As if a light bulb had gone off over everyone's head, Eileen knew Ruth and Dorothy were both right on target. "So what we need is quiet time alone."

"Or at least time away from watchful eyes," Dorothy said.

Sally May muffled a laugh. "Like that's going to happen in Tuckers Bluff."

"Okay," Eileen conceded. "Maybe not *alone* alone. Maybe all we need is just sort of alone."

"Sort of alone?" women's voices echoed.

Smiling, Eileen nodded her head. "Yep, and I know just where to start."

• • • •

"It was really nice of Allison and Hannah to invite Sarah to visit the stables this afternoon with the big girls."

"I know there's nothing Hannah loves more than kids and horses. And she loves teaching the young ones before they learn fear."

"Well, it worked out perfectly since your Aunt Eileen suggested to Jamie we go look in his attic this afternoon. I've been a little worried about how to make everything work. We lost so much."

Reed bit down on his back teeth, then smiled. "Things can only get better now."

"That's what I keep saying, which is why I'm so thankful for the Farradays." Not that Chloe should've been surprised. Whether born into the clan or married into the clan, the Farradays always seem to have each other's back. And apparently, while she lived in their home, she and her daughters were family and would have plenty of people to watch out for them.

Reed pulled into the parking lot for the pub. "It doesn't hurt that Sarah seems quite fond of horses."

"I know!" Chloe twisted in her seat to face him. "I wasn't surprised how excited she was about the newborn horse, but I thought she'd be afraid of the big ones."

"Nope." Reed chuckled. "Like it or not you have a horsewoman on your hands."

Facing forward again, Chloe shook her head. "I have no idea where she got that from. I mean, I'm not afraid of horses, but I'm a city girl. And even though Pat was a native Texan, I don't think suburban Dallas counts as horse country."

His face still painted with amusement, Reed undid his safety belt and faced her. "Maybe it's in the water."

It was nice to laugh. She hadn't done much of it the last few days, or weeks, or months for that matter, but when she did, Reed usually had something to do with it. "Maybe."

Inside O'Farraedeigh's, Jamie sat at a high-top, his fingers clacking away at the computer. As daylight from the door shined in his direction, Jamie looked up at them. "Hi. Glad you could make it."

"It's very generous of you to offer for me to look around your attic."

"When I bought the place all I wanted was the building. All the stuff stored upstairs was an unexpected bonus. Abby and I have picked through the things we'd like to use and I simply don't have the heart to throw out the remainder. You're actually doing me a favor by taking some of this stuff off my hands." Chuckling, he pushed to his feet. "Heck, the best thing you could do for me is take it all off my hands."

Taking it all might be a bit much. Her house was just fine for the three of them but it wasn't huge. Smiling politely, she followed in Jamie's wake, Reed on her heels.

"Watch your step. I haven't had a chance to sort through yesterday's deliveries." Jamie stopped at the foot of the staircase. "It's all up this way. The loft area goes all the way to the back of the building. There should be a narrow path for the most part, but feel free to move anything out of your way if you need to."

"Thank you." Chloe's gaze lifted to the top of the stairs and glancing back, quickly calculated just how much space there was up there. She'd expected a handful of old pieces stuffed in a corner. Slowly making her way up the stairs, she had a feeling this was going to be more like a furniture warehouse. "Oh, my."

Reed nodded. "Yeah. I'm sure there are antique dealers who would gladly kill to have their pick of some of this *stuff*."

Softly her fingers brushed across the top of an old dresser. Slightly dusty, she had the impression that it had been cleaned and polished not that long ago. "This is not what I was expecting."

Reed's smile slipped. "You don't like antiques?"

She quickly spun around to face him. "No. I love the craftsmanship of real antiques. I guess somewhere in the back of my mind I did not realize when they said antiques they meant *antiques*."

The smile back on his face, Reed waved a hand from her toward the back. "How do you want to tackle this? Front to back, back to front, together, or divide and conquer?"

Suddenly she felt a tad overwhelmed. Her mind quickly scrambling through which pieces had been completely ruined, and if Jamie was telling the truth, she let herself imagine the empty spaces where she often told herself some day she could afford a nice piece to fill the spot. "I think I'd like to do this together, please."

"Then let's have at it. I suggest back to front. This way, we can get a feel for what is up here as we walk by, and then take your time with things you find interesting."

Chloe nodded. It had been a very long time since she'd had any help adulting. If she wasn't careful, she might get used to it.

Holding one of her hands, and his other hand at the small of her back, he gently led her through the maze of boxes, trunks, and pieces varying from needlepoint foot stools to massive armoires. Suddenly his hand tugged her to a stop. "Careful."

Her foot bumping into a hard surface, she tripped back against him. His grip tightened to study her. "Sorry. I was distracted by that table over there. I guess I didn't see where I was going."

"No problem. Let's check it out."

"I don't really have space for a table. When Pat and I bought the house, we'd hoped to one day add on."

Reaching the table, she counted the chairs stacked atop it. "I always wanted a dining room to hold a set like this. My Nana had a table in her dining room. Even though we were a small family, I think she always hoped it would grow." Chloe chuckled. "She probably prayed every night for me to find a nice Irish Catholic boy and have a dozen children."

"What happened to the table?"

"When she and my grandfather decided it was time to downsize, Pat and I hadn't been married very long. We were living in base housing and I couldn't imagine ever having room for a table of that size. I think she sold it to a distant cousin."

"These chairs are in pretty good shape." Having pulled one to the floor, he pushed and leaned before taking a seat. "Seat's more comfortable than I expected. Maybe now with the insurance would be a good time to bump out the house? Get your table?"

She shook her head. "No. It would be weird doing things Pat and I planned without Pat."

"Why?" He sighed and rolled his eyes heavenward. "Sorry, what I mean is, if it's something you really wanted, do you think Pat would be upset if you did it without him?"

Tearing her gaze away from Reed, or maybe from the question, she stared at the table and chairs. "It's a nice set."

He nodded, but said nothing. He was making her think. Think about things she'd spent a long time avoiding.

"No. He wouldn't be upset."

"For what it's worth, I think he'd want you to have everything y'all dreamed of."

Keeping her gaze on the table, she nodded.

"Hey." Reed tipped his head, waiting till she looked at him. "I don't know a lot, but I'm sure of one thing. He'd want you to be happy."

"Yes. He would." She blinked back a tear, and forced herself to turn away, redirecting her attention to a dresser across the way. "The girls are sharing a dresser. I could use another one."

And just like that she did as she'd always done. Trudged ahead, moving on. Sort of. Stealing a quick glance over her shoulder, she gave the dining room set one last look. If she wanted to make any of those some days happen, she was going to have to make some changes.

"Is this what you mean?" Reed stopped by a pair of heavy oak dressers.

"Yes. Yes, it is." She plastered on a smile. Already things were turning around. And why didn't it surprise her that like every other good thing that happened to her in recent years, Reed was here to help.

• • • •

"Man, this is good." Reed loved the pub's corned beef and cabbage.

With a lazy shrug, Jamie waved his hands at him. "I wish I could take the credit. But I swear it's that pot of Aunt Eileen's. I don't know if it's love, magic, or decades of seasoning, but no matter which new pot I try, it never tastes the same as with the family pot."

"I vote for all three." Chloe wiped the corners of her mouth with her napkin. "And I'm with Reed. Nobody boils corned beef and cabbage like this."

Watching Chloe, Reed couldn't make up his mind if something had shifted and she seemed more content, or if perhaps it was merely wishful thinking on his part. But the weight of all the bad things that had happened in her life seemed to have lifted and the gal in front of him reminded him of the one he'd met in a different pub so many years ago.

"All right then." Jamie took a step back. "I have a few things to do before we open the doors tonight. Just let me know when you'll be picking up your new furnishings."

"Thanks again."

"Our pleasure."

Chloe kept her eyes on him until Jamie disappeared down a hall. "I like that."

Any other woman and he might have thought she meant Jamie. Try as he might, he had no idea what she was talking about. For a split moment he wondered if he would ever understand women. "Like what?"

"The way he said *our*. He and Abby make such a cute couple."

He hadn't really given it any thought. All the Farradays seemed well suited to their mates.

The sound of Christmas carols from the sidewalk drifted inside and Chloe hummed along. "This is one of my favorites."

"Mine too." His fingers began tapping to the rhythm of the song. "For a while there all they played was the jazzed up contemporary version. I missed the more original interpretations."

"I know!" Beaming, she dropped her fork and eagerly leaned forward. "It drove me crazy every time that jazzy version came on the car radio."

For the next few minutes, only every other word she said registered. He couldn't get over how for the first time in a very long time Chloe seemed so lighthearted, happily chatting away. There was no sign of the reserved woman he'd come to know the last couple of years.

"Oh, look." Chloe pointed to the opposite corner of the pub where Jamie lifted a tree section from a large box. "He's decorating." Her gaze dropped to her wrist. "We don't have to pick Sarah up for a while yet. Do you think he'd mind if we helped?"

Even if Jamie did mind, which was doubtful, to keep that beautiful smile on her face Reed would have sold his soul to let her help. "Let's find out."

It didn't take much convincing for Jamie to accept the help.

As Chloe opened each of the ornament boxes, her face beaming with every discovery, Reed couldn't think of anything he'd rather be doing.

"Oh wow. They saved the tinsel." Sitting on the floor, she held up a Christmas card with tinsel tucked inside. "This is the old stuff that really sparkles. When I was a kid, after Christmas we'd take the tinsel off the tree, wad it up, and have indoor snowball fights."

"Bet your folks just loved that."

"They looked the other way. Pat and I used to do the same thing, but with my snowball ornaments. It was silly and childish but we loved it."

"Snowball? Like frozen water that melts?" Of course he knew she had to mean something else, but he was enjoying the light in her eyes as she went down memory lane. Before today, it had been a long time since they'd talked about life with Pat. It was almost like the only way she knew to avoid the hurt was to avoid his memory, and now she seemed almost at peace remembering.

"Yeah." She reached for another ornament. "I liked making holiday crafts. I would crotchet small balls, fill them with cotton, and then glue on sparkly things. Of course, after a few years of taking-down-the-tree snowball fights, most of the sparkles had come off."

"Sounds like fun."

A sweet smile teased one side of her mouth as she leaned back. "It was."

Memories of years of friendship came flooding back. "The year we were deployed over Christmas, Pat would talk for hours about shopping together, decorating the tree, and how his favorite part of stringing popcorn was eating every other piece."

Her soft laugh filled the room. "I always had to pop twice as many bags. Sometimes he was more of a kid than Emmie."

"Maybe. Christmas brings out the little kid in all of us."

She pushed to her feet and let out a sigh. "I've been a little remiss on that recently, but fire or no fire, I'm going to fix it. This year Christmas will be merry."

"That's my girl." He'd meant it in the simplest of way, but surprised himself at how much he liked the sound of it. Through the years Chloe had quickly gone from the girl-that-got-away to his buddy's wife. No man ever dared poach on a buddy's girl and certainly not his wife. Keeping his smile simple, he turned to grab another box. She may not be his buddy's wife anymore, but she wasn't his girl either.

He heard one of the chairs dragging across the floor, and turned back. A box in one hand, a foot on the seat, and the other hand on the seatback, Chloe was just about to hoist herself up. "What are you doing?"

"You have to start decorating from the top down."

"I know that, but you could get hurt."

Her eyes popped open wide. "It's a chair, not a foxhole."

"Still. They're designed to sit in. Not stand on." He reached for the chair. "I'm sure Jamie has a ladder I can use."

"You?" Her spine snapped stiff. "I hate to break it to you, but I have been climbing chairs and ladders and changing lightbulbs and hanging pictures and all sorts of hazardous duty all by myself for over two years. I'm pretty sure I can handle hanging a few ornaments."

If he wasn't a mistaken, this might just be their very first fight. The idea almost made him laugh. As cute as she looked all fired up, she also looked ready to slug him for getting in her way. And she did have a point. Decorating a tree wasn't quite the same as climbing on a roof and fixing a chimney. "You're right. I'm sorry. But at least let me see if Jamie has a ladder. It would be much easier than standing on a chair."

The twinkle sparkled in her eye again and the tips of her pretty mouth tipped up into a sweet smile. "No, I'm the one who owes you an apology. I overreacted. I'm sorry. Let me go see if there's a ladder around." She set an ornament back in the box, maneuvered around him, and paused to place a quick kiss on his cheek. "You're a nice man, Reed Taylor. Thank you."

Stunned silent, he nodded and watched her scurry over to where Jamie stood behind the bar. *Nice man*. What he didn't know was if he had been relegated to the category of nice like a new puppy, or nice like a knight on a white horse. Maybe, just maybe, he wanted to be somewhere in between.

CHAPTER EIGHT

The bell rang over the door to Sisters. Chloe loved the sound of it. For some reason it always made her feel like she was stepping back in time to a simpler easier way of life. Some days she expected to see Ma or Pa Ingalls come through the door, or Mrs. Oleson come out from behind the curtain separating the store from the offices. Today it was Sister who stepped out to greet her.

"Good morning to you." The shorter blonde, who clearly believed the bigger the hair the closer to God, came over sporting a sunny grin. "It's so good to see you." She leaned over and handed a peppermint stick to Sarah. "And you too, little lady."

"What do we say?"

Tucked behind her mother's leg, Sarah spied the offered gift carefully before venturing out and snatching it up. "Tank you."

"You're very welcome." Sister straightened to what there was of her full height, then excused herself to answer the phone.

List in hand, Chloe walked over to the toy section. She already knew what gifts she wanted for all the Farraday grands, she just had to budget carefully. Sifting through the best choices, she set two aside and considered a third. Sarah entertained herself inspecting the shoe department. The kid was fascinated with shoes. Good thing too, Sarah's distraction made it easy for Chloe to look around. She'd managed to check a few things off her list by the time Sister came by to help.

"I hear things are moving along well with your house." Sister smiled up at her.

Chloe glanced around the store. She had one more person on her list and no clue what to get him. "Well, they *were*."

"Oh, dear. Were? That doesn't sound good."

She should have realized that any foray into town, whether at the café or the hairdressers, the Sisters would require updates on her home's reconstruction. "The demolition of all the damage went fairly quickly. But the reconstruction has hit a few snags."

Sissy, the sibling who had clearly inherited all of her traits from the opposite parent as her sister, came out from the back offices smiling. "What's this I hear about snags?"

Sister waved a finger in her direction. "Chloe was just telling me about the delays on her house."

"Oh, no." Sissy's lips pressed tightly together. "I thought Sean was being a tad optimistic about getting Patrick and his crew down here."

"You know about that?" she asked.

Both sisters waved her off as if she had just asked what color was the sky, but Sissy spoke up. "Patrick Farraday hasn't set foot in this town in over twenty years. None of us know what happened, though we do know on occasion the cousins still speak to each other."

"Yes," Sister agreed. "On occasion."

The little said around the house had given Chloe the impression Uncle Patrick was a brother. "Cousins?"

Sister bobbed her head. "Brian and Patrick are brothers, so Patrick is Sean's cousin just like Hannah, Ian, and Jamison's dad."

That made sense. She hadn't wanted to ask, and very little was being said about it at the house. After all, everyone actually *in* the Farraday family knew the history and had no reason to explain. All she knew is that Uncle Patrick agreed to try, but so far he'd been unable to bring a crew down from Oklahoma.

The bell rang again and everyone turned to look. A smile tugged at her cheeks the moment Reed came through the door.

"I thought that was your car."

"Unkie." All of Sarah's shyness melted away and she flung her arms at Reed.

Well practiced after two weeks of Sarah hanging on to him every chance she got, without looking, he leaned in her direction so she could crawl up onto his hip.

"Are you here for that package?" Sister asked over her shoulder as she hurried behind the counter. "It came first thing this morning as promised. Exactly what Sam ordered."

"Perfect." His smile grew wider as he held Sarah with one arm and accepted a small box with the other.

This last week had flown by. Both the girls had adapted to life at the ranch. Chloe had to admit, there were times when she forgot that she was an introvert by nature and not a Farraday by birth. The more she did with Aunt Eileen and her friends and family, the more Chloe wondered what had possessed her to lock herself away from the town after Pat died.

"I'm glad I caught you." Reed shifted Sarah to sit on his shoulders and she giggled with delight.

Chloe tried not to laugh too hard when Sarah wrapped her hands around his mouth then eyes.

"What did we say?" he asked Sarah.

Without a word, her daughter leaned forward and dropped her hands below his chin. For now that was fine, but Chloe wondered what he was going to do when that too became a strangling grip. Not that it mattered. So far he'd handled parenting like a pro. It was one of the things she loved about him. That and his endearing lost boy look. Watching him laugh and tickle her little girl, making her feel more and more at ease with the new normal, then glance over at Chloe and wink, making sure she didn't feel left out. How could any woman resist a guy like that? And why would they want to?

• • • •

Reed followed behind Chloe. It had been a few days since she'd seen the work on the house and she really wanted to go look. He wasn't sure he'd ever fully understand women. One minute she was smiling, enjoying the playful moment with him and her daughter, then a far away look came over her face and she was rushing off, almost desperate to stop at her house on the way to the Farradays. There was no way he was letting her face whatever had changed her mood alone. So here he was riding on her six.

The front of the house looked much the same as it had the first time they'd seen it after the fire. All the volunteers had focused on repairing the roof and the exterior walls first. The roof had taken longer than they'd anticipated due to both a delay in supplies arriving and the shortage of free hands.

Chloe exited her car, and by the time she had retrieved Sarah from the car seat, Reed stood at her side. "Ready?" he asked.

"Maybe, maybe not. But let's not let that stop me."

"Fair enough." As far as he was concerned, Chloe was one-of-a-kind. Tough, brave, and incredibly devoted, all wrapped up in a sweet, caring, and of course beautiful package.

The minute they crossed the threshold, Chloe stopped to catch her breath. No way of knowing if that was a good or bad thing. "You doing okay?"

Holding Sarah's hand, she slowly moved forward. "It looks so different."

Since she'd last been here, they had redone the roof and completely rebuilt the exterior walls. Now when you walked inside, instead of the eye going straight across and out to the backyard, it stopped at the studded wall. The exterior of the house was still wrapped in weatherproofing waiting for the cement board siding, but that could be done later. Until today the interior had been a priority on steroids.

"Without furniture or cabinets, it looks so big. So different." Her eyes slowly scanned every corner.

"The header separating the living from dining is gone. Turns out it was only decorative. That helps the space look bigger too."

"It really does." They walked through every room on the first floor before climbing upstairs. Chloe slowly made her way down the hall to the girls' room.

He wasn't positive, but he thought he saw her hand shake as her fingers clutched the knob and turned it, shoving the door open.

The girls' room, like Chloe's downstairs, already had new sheetrock which went a long way to making it look more finished than the living room and kitchen.

"I'm sorry we couldn't get it done in time."

She shook her head and tugged her fidgety daughter closer. "Don't be. I've watched enough remodeling shows to know even with a huge crew they always need at least six weeks."

"Then you're not disappointed?" He resisted the urge to cross the room, stand beside her, tuck his finger under her chin and just watch her eyes. But he was better off keeping his hands in his pockets. The temptation to touch was getting more and more difficult to ignore.

"The whole town has gone out of their way to give me a home for Christmas. They gave up all their free time and used every connection possible to speed up the process. How could I possibly be disappointed in that?"

Sarah broke free of her mother's grip and ran toward him, wrapping herself around his leg.

"Hey, sweetie. Do you like how your room is coming along?"

Much like she'd done that first week after the fire, Sarah buried her head in his shoulder.

Quickly crossing the room, Chloe brushed a lock of her daughter's hair away from her face and tucked it behind her ear. "Have you picked a color for the walls yet?"

Her chin tucked into her neck, Sarah shook her head.

"I was thinking pink would be nice." Not that he had any interest in pink, but he was pretty sure it was the favorite color of every female under the age of ten.

Apparently he was on the right track. Sarah lifted her chin, tilted her head, and seemed to be checking out the walls.

"Or maybe flowers?" he asked. "I've seen some pretty wallpaper with flowers. Which flowers do you like?"

Now Sarah was sitting upright and looking around. Finally she pushed back to look Reed in the face. "Yellow."

He felt his cheeks pull into a wide smile. "Then yellow it will be."

Chloe patted her daughter's back. "If Emmie agrees. She gets to pick too."

"Yellow," Sarah repeated, back to the happy, playful girl of a short while ago. It was taking time, but Sarah seemed to be adjusting a bit more every day, and he hoped he had at least a little to do with it.

"We may have to pull off a Solomon," he suggested. "You know, split the room down the middle. One half yellow and the other half... who knows."

The twinkle was back in Chloe's eyes. "Sounds like we have a plan."

"Then you're okay with celebrating the holidays at the ranch?"

"And with you?"

The question took him by surprise. She wanted him to share Christmas with her and the kids. There had been two holiday seasons since they'd lost Pat, and this was the first time she'd even suggested including him. How crazy was he that her wanting him to be part of her family this Christmas made his brain go soft with thoughts of flowers, the real kind, and moonlight and, heaven help him—love?

CHAPTER NINE

"I can't believe it's Christmas Eve already." Eileen pulled out a bin filled with cookie cutters. "Where has the time gone? We have so much work to do."

Chloe hadn't baked cookies from scratch since she was a little girl visiting her grandmother. "Just tell me what you need me to do."

"Here we are." Catherine came in through the back door, her husband Connor on one side and her daughter Stacey squeezing between them, making a beeline inside. "Don't run in the house."

Connor let out a small burst of laughter. "Like that rule will ever be upheld. This is grandma and grandpa's house now. There are no rules."

"There are some." Eileen waved a rolling pin at her nephew. "And speaking of grandparents, you two are behind the curve on babies."

Catherine coughed on air, and Connor's eyes nearly popped from their sockets. Quickly jumping to their defense, Toni, Joanna, Grace and Hannah all called out a censuring "Aunt Eileen" from the dining room.

Handing Chloe several boxes of butter, Becky shook her head. "Don't mind them. Aunt Eileen has been on a more-babies kick for months. We've all gotten used to it."

"Babies are nice." Chloe shrugged.

"See!" Aunt Eileen hollered over her shoulder from where she stood by the sink. "She's on my side." Under her breath she mumbled, "Too bad I'm out of nephews."

One foot in the kitchen, Meg, reversed course and retreated to safety in the living room. The sound of a *Toy Story* movie traveled to the kitchen between snippets of chatter and bursts of laughter from the rest of the family and the children. The entire chaotic scenario brought a smile to Chloe's lips. She was learning to like chaos.

"Who wants to help with the reindeer cookies?" Aunt Eileen called into the living room then turned to Chloe. "Baking Christmas cookies is meant to be done with children."

Which is why Chloe was glad that her house was no longer scheduled to be move-in ready after all. Emmie would have missed out on all the cookie fun and general miscellaneous shenanigans if they'd been home. And so would she.

The back door squeaked opened again. The sight of Reed entering the kitchen, all smiles, made Chloe's insides flutter like a flustered teen. Something had shifted that day decorating the tree at Jamie's pub, then at Sisters it hit her she just might be an idiot. She'd made her mind up walking the half-done house. The house that had long ago ceased to be a home. Taking a slow look at the life she'd been hiding from. Reed Taylor was someone special and she was done taking his being in her life for granted.

"Afternoon." Just like the other Farraday men, Reed paused to clean off his boots before stepping inside. Somehow, even that routine habit made her grin even wider. She was well past smitten.

Her little one with bionic ears, who seemed almost miraculously back to her pre-fire self, sprinted into the kitchen with only his single word greeting as a starting pistol. "Unkie. Can we go look at the baby horses?"

Reed looked to Aunt Eileen who nodded, then to Chloe before agreeing. "We should check if the other kids want to come." The guy was batting a thousand. His continued thoughtfulness had her cheeks almost hurting from so much smiling.

"If you're taking all the kids you'll need back up." Aunt Eileen looked over her shoulder at him, a sly grin slid into place and quickly disappeared. "Chloe, you up for it?"

"Yes, ma'am." She pushed away from the counter she'd been leaning against. "I'll check in the living room."

The coffee table, game table, and multiple patches of ground space were covered with wrapping paper of varying colors, scissors, and tape. Each child had one or two adults dedicated to helping them wrap presents. From the abandoned station she could see even Emmie had been working on a gift. Looking at the floor to ceiling tree tucked in one corner, already perched on a sea of beautifully wrapped gifts, she had no idea where they were going to fit anymore.

"Uncle Reed and Sarah are going outside to see the foals. Anyone want to tag along?" she asked.

To her surprise, all five children sprang up. The youngest, Brooks' little girl, with a bit less speed than the older ones.

"Need some help?" Ethan asked. He and Brooks started to stand.

"Nope." She waved for them to stay seated. "Two adults and five children. We should have this."

Sean chuckled under his breath. "Just remember, anything more than two kids and you'll always be one arm or one parent short."

There was probably more truth in that statement than she wanted to ponder at this particular moment in time. "Thanks. I'll keep that in mind."

"You do that." The family patriarch smiled the kind of grin that made his eyes sparkle.

Chloe and Reed had barely made it out the back door when Finn came rushing past them and leapt off the back porch before spinning around to face them and the children. He called out, "Last one inside is a rotten egg," then trotted to the barn.

Oh that was so not what they needed now. Sarah turned squiggly in Reed's arms and within seconds all five children were happily chasing after Finn.

Shaking her head, Chloe couldn't decide if she should laugh it off or run like hell to catch up. "That man had better not take Aunt Eileen up on her pleas for more grandchildren until he's matured just a little bit more."

"Actually, he's really good with kids. His ability to become almost childlike makes him a favorite amongst the next generation of cousins."

"I can see why."

Reed laughed. "Come on. Let's see what comes of this." And then he surprised the dickens out of her by offering his hand. Not just a polite help her getting down the stairs gesture, but a walk with me and I hope my palms don't sweat kind of hand-holding.

Heaven help her. She finally gets to hold hands with a nice guy who makes her heart flutter with only a smile and her mind runs straight to sweating palms. How unromantic was that?

"You're thinking too hard."

"I'm sorry, what?" She missed a step.

"Careful." Reed's grip on her tightened. "There's a little frown across your forehead. The one that often makes an appearance when you're concentrating on how to solve a problem."

She raised her hand to her face and ran her fingers along her forehead. "Sorry. Just thinking. It's stupid."

"There's nothing stupid about the way you think." They'd reached the barn door and his pace slowed, then came to a stop just before bringing the inside into view. "There's something I've been meaning to say for a while and I need to get it out."

"Of course. Shoot." She tried not to fidget like her youngest daughter or let her mind run off with worst case scenarios. Not now. Not when things were finally looking up.

Still holding her hand, he spun her around to face him and grabbed the other hand. Stepping in toe to toe, he slowly lowered his head, and just as his lips could almost reach hers, he murmured, "This."

His mouth descended on hers, not like the quick peck the last time they were caught under the mistletoe, but a real honest to goodness, this man is really into this woman, kind of kiss.

Not till this very second when she melted against him did she realize just how long she'd been waiting for this. A kiss. And not just any kiss, but a real kiss from the one and only Reed Taylor.

• • • •

The last thing Reed wanted to do was let go of this woman. The taste of her on his lips and the feel of her in his arms was everything he'd been dreaming of. But they had multiple children they were responsible for and poor Finn didn't have five arms.

Wishing he didn't have to, he pulled back. Still holding her hands, he let his forehead briefly touch hers. "Can I have a rain check?"

Her head gently moved up then down. "Absolutely."

Slowly he eased back another step then like a couple of kids on a first date, strolled the rest of the distance to where the horses lived. The barnyard tour was a big hit with the kids. He suspected no matter how much time they spent in a barn, experiencing the playfulness of a newborn foal would be something none of these west Texas bred kids were likely to grow tired of. At least two or three times he managed to work in that they were under mistletoe, knowing full well the kids would point back to him and he'd get an authorized excuse for one more tiny kiss. Bless whoever had gone crazy with the mistletoe in the stables.

"Oh, good. Everyone's back." Aunt Eileen watched the parade of children and adults march in through the kitchen door with so much joy on her face that Reed hoped she got at least one more of those grandbabies she wanted. "Now remember the rules. As soon as the last batch of cookies is out of the oven we all get to open one present."

Squeals of delight filled the room as children scattered about the massive kitchen table establishing their stations. Parents worked with their children. Since Chloe was the only one with two children and one parent, Reed happily stepped in to work with Sarah. Things had been slowly changing the last few weeks, but this morning he felt the world shift to a new and sweeter future. Now more than before he was positive at least one thing he'd bought for Chloe was the right choice.

"Here we go." Aunt Eileen placed the first cooled batch on the table.

"I love gingerbread men," Catherine cooed.

"Oh, no." Aunt Eileen walked beside her and flipped the man upside down. "We're decorating reindeer."

Reed took another look. He was with Catherine. All he saw was an upside down man. Twenty minutes later the kids were covered in icing and powdered sugar and laughing and smiling, and sure enough, the upside down men had become antlered reindeer cookies.

"Coffee anyone?" Chloe carried a tray of mugs in one hand and a carafe of hot coffee in the other. When she walked past Stacey's station, her mom's eyes grew round as circles.

"Excuse me." Catherine bolted upright and hurried away from the kitchen.

From the corner of his eye, Reed noticed Connor's attention land on his wife moments before following after her. *Interesting*.

A scratching sound at the back door distracted everyone from the next batch of cookies. This time they were cutting out stars and Santas and Christmas trees.

"Stacey, honey, would you let the dog in?" Aunt Eileen laid a blob of dough in front of the two oldest girls with a rolling pin, and paused at Stacey's station. "Where'd your mom go?"

The little girl shrugged and opened the door. Gray came hurrying in, something colorful clutched in his mouth. Reed seemed to be the only one who saw it. Everyone else was busy in their assigned baking tasks, completely ignoring the large dog.

"Sorry we're late." Meg dropped a bag by the door and hurried into the kitchen to hug all the women. "What time is dinner?"

"Dinner?" Aunt Eileen looked up. "We just had lunch."

"Not really," Becky answered. "Lunch was almost two hours ago."

Aunt Eileen set the wooden spoon in a mixing bowl and hefted both her hands on her hips. "That's hardly time for dinner."

Repositioning herself with a mixing bowl, she shook her head and smiled. "You have a couple of cookies for a snack. The reindeer will go nice with a little ice cream if you're really hungry."

Meg cast a glance around the table at the decorated cookies, nodding her head. A bowl in hand, she scooped out some vanilla ice cream. "Anyone else want some?"

A chorus of *no thank yous* rounded the table.

Helping Sarah roll out the cut edges of leftover dough into a new clean section for more cookies, he could hear Meg shuffling things around in the pantry.

"What are you doing in there? Redecorating?" Aunt Eileen called out without looking up.

"Nothing," Meg answered, still in the pantry. It was a few more minutes before she emerged with only the bowl in her hand and a smile on her face. Whatever she'd hunted for she'd obviously found.

Mouth empty, Gray scratched to be let out, and as Emmie opened the door this time, Gray trotted out and the other dog pranced in. Once again, the animal had something in her mouth just like Gray but from where he stood Reed couldn't make out what the dog's favorite toy was.

By the time the last batch of cookies was done, a few of the men had joined in on the fun, Declan and Abby had been the last family to arrive, the dogs had made carrying things in and out of the house a regular routine, Meg had just made her third trip for ice cream, and pretty much everyone, child and adult alike, was covered in flour. All in all, a very successful day.

"I'd say it's time to clean up and then we can do our gift exchange before the Christmas Eve Parade." Aunt Eileen dusted flour from her hands and surveying her clan, grinned. "It's going to be the best Christmas ever."

Never had he seen children and adults alike move so fast. With dishes of cookies scattered around the cozy family room, everyone had taken their seats, coupled off. Reed watched each waiting couple as they placed gifts under the tree and pulled a single one to share. Even though this wasn't his first family event at the ranch, having Chloe sitting beside him with Emmie and Sarah on either side, he finally understood why the Farradays were always so blasted happy.

"Here we go." Aunt Eileen slapped her hands together, rubbing enthusiastically.

Grinning from ear to ear, Sarah sprang up and shoved a small gift in Reed's hands. "Your turn."

Aunt Eileen chuckled. "Guess, we start with you Reed."

Looking around, he felt a bit self-conscious. After all, he wasn't even a Farraday, but there was no refusing the excited grin on little Sarah's face. As slowly as he could without dragging it out, he tore the paper off and uncovered a dark wood frame. Inside, a photo of Sarah on his shoulders, laughing and him listening intently to something Emmie was saying. Saliva dried up in his mouth and he struggled to swallow. "I love it."

Chloe held a timid smile. "I snapped it on the spur of the moment and, it just seemed like the right gift from us."

"It's perfect." He hugged to the two girls at his side, smiled at Chloe, and asked, "Who's next?"

"Might as well start with the first born." Eileen gestured across the way. "Adam?"

An arm slung around his wife, Adam gave her a kiss on the temple and seemed for the first time to look down at her bowl. "Good heavens, what is that?"

"Ice cream." Meg smiled.

"It's green." Adam's eyes were big and round with surprise or disgust. Reed wasn't sure which.

"Yes." She smiled brighter. "It is."

Sitting on her other side, Connor leaned over to peek. "Oh, hell. I'm with my brother. What is that?"

"I told you. Ice cream." Meg's smile slipped. "Where's your present?" Dish in hand, she leaned forward to pick up a small gift and set the dish on the coffee table.

The only problem Reed could see was on its way to the table, the ice cream concocted bowl came too close to Catherine, who took one whiff, sprang to her feet, and ran out of the room.

All eyes darted from Catherine, to Meg, to the dish, and up at Connor who had taken off after his wife.

The only one frowning was Aunt Eileen. "Something's up and I want to know what it is."

"Mrs. Toe," Emmie answered.

Aunt Eileen shot the little girl a sweet smile.

"See." Emmie pointed to the lone sprig of mistletoe in the house. Directly in front of the Christmas tree.

"Thank you, sweetie." Aunt Eileen held her smile and startled with surprise when Gray dragged a laundry basket into the room and pretty much dropped it, not at, but on her feet. "Good heavens. What are you doing?"

"Uh oh." Someone muttered from across the room.

Catherine came back into the den. "Sorry folks. I guess we have something to share."

Grinning like a loon, Aunt Eileen lifted a small square patch with the same colors he'd seen Gray carrying earlier in the day. "Would it have anything to do with this?"

"What's that?" Catherine squinted.

The smile on Aunt Eileen's face shifted to a look of confusion. "Judging by the pastel shades of yarn and the traditional zig zag shape, my guess is the start of a baby blanket."

Catherine's eyes widened. "Whose?"

"I thought," Aunt Eileen stared at her niece-in-law, "yours."

"Not mine." She shook her head. "Crafts and I don't get along"

"But you were about to tell us you're pregnant?"

His arm already hanging protectively around his wife, Connor grinned and nodded. "We are."

Shouts of *yay* and *congrats* and a few *wows* carried through the room. Instantly folks jumped up to hug and cheer on the soon to be new parents.

A sharp whistle broke the cheerful chaos. Aunt Eileen stood

with a pinky hanging from each corner of her mouth. Reaching behind her, she lifted the blanket up for all to see.

"I don't suppose," Catherine looked to Meg, "it has anything to do with the pickles in your ice cream?"

"Pickles?"

Reed wasn't sure which of the ladies had muttered the word with so much disgust. But from the looks on several faces, it could have been anyone.

Letting out a sigh, Meg placed a hand on her husband's knee and smiled. "Surprise."

From the way Adam's eyes sprang open, Reed was pretty sure the revelation was as new to him as it was to everyone else in the room. Before anybody could react, he'd grabbed his wife in a strangled hug and twirled her around.

"Whoa, cowboy," Meg shouted. "Unless you want to be covered in pickles and vanilla ice cream you may not want to do that again."

"Oh my gosh. I'm so sorry." Flustered, Adam patted her shoulders as if steadying a nervous filly. "Are you okay?"

Smiling, she nodded. "And hungry."

Gray barked and Aunt Eileen looked down. He'd lifted another item from the basket. A ball of blue yarn with the beginnings of something dangling from the string.

Holding the item up, Aunt Eileen looked to Catherine. "Yours?"

Connor's wife shook her head.

Spinning slightly, she waved it at Meg. "You?"

Like her sister-in-law, Meg shook her head.

A slow smile took over Eileen's face. "Okay, who's going to fess up?"

Eyes surveyed the room, looking at each other, when very slowly one hand inched its way up.

"That," Becky said softly, "would be mine. Grams is teaching me to make booties. But what I don't understand is how did Gray get into my knitting bag in the car?"

"Who knows?" His arm looped around his wife's waist, DJ chuckled. "It's Gray."

"True." Sean agreed with a nod.

"So this," Aunt Eileen lifted a needlepoint work in its hoop from the basket and waved it between Meg and Catherine, "must belong to one of you two."

No one, especially not Reed, expected both heads to shake from side to side.

"No?" Aunt Eileen whispered. "I think I need to sit down."

The woman practically fell into the seat behind her. Startled by the dazed look on her face, pretty much everyone in the room forgot about the impending baby news and migrated toward their aunt.

When Brooks grabbed her wrist, she seemed to snap out of the fog. "I'm all right. But who does this," she waved the needlepoint in the air, "belong to?"

From where Reed sat, he could hear the heavy sigh from the edges of the crowd seconds before Jamie and Abby's fingers linked tightly together.

"That would be us," Abby said.

"Oh my Lord." Aunt Eileen held her hand to her heart. "Four. We're having four grandbabies?"

Several heads bobbed and Eileen's eyes suddenly flashed big and round. "Anyone else?"

Sean laughed. "Good grief, woman. Isn't four enough for you?"

Joining in the laughter, she smacked her husband playfully on the arm. "I'm just checking."

As if on cue, the other dog stuck his muzzle into the basket and lifted out a rattle.

"I'm not so sure about this," Aunt Eileen said softly.

All eyes followed the dog as it looked up at Eileen and looking left then right, moved forward. When he stopped in front of Chloe, Reed's heart began to race.

No one in the room was more surprised than Chloe when the

small wooden rattle landed in her lap. Eyes wide, she shook her head rapidly. "Don't look at me. As far as I know there haven't been any new bright stars rising in the North."

The startled joke about the immaculate conception eased the tensions and made everybody chuckle.

Slapping her hands on her thighs, Aunt Eileen pushed to her feet. "Well," she looked to Chloe, "this wouldn't be the first time the dogs knew something none of us did." She dipped her chin once and slapped her hands at her sides. "I don't know about anyone else, but I think it's time for a celebratory drink." Casting her gaze in the direction of the four pregnant women, she smiled. "Non-alcoholic, of course. Then off to the parade."

Sean reached for his wife's hand. "It's going to be one heck of a Christmas."

Leaning into her husband, Aunt Eileen nodded. "I'll see your Christmas and raise you one heck of a great year."

CHAPTER TEN - EPILOGUE

"**W**here do you want these?" Holding two quilts, Reed stood staring at Chloe as if she were the only woman on the planet. "Back in the closet or on the girls' beds?"

Slowly inching forward, Chloe touched each one of the beloved blankets with the respect an aged piece of American craftsmanship deserved. "I think it's time they go on the beds."

"On the beds it is." He leaned forward and gave her gentle kiss on the nose.

For a split second Morgan wasn't sure either one was going to move, when finally Reed took a step back and marched upstairs.

"You two do that a lot, don't you?" he asked.

"Hmm?" Chloe dragged her gaze away from the stairs and faced Morgan. "Sorry, what?"

Chuckling to himself, he shook his head. "Never mind." Ever since he and his brothers had arrived the day after Christmas, Reed and Chloe had been making doe eyes at each other or stealing kisses in different corners of this house and the ranch.

"Have I said thank you yet?"

Morgan's brother Quinn paused as he walked by and tipped his head near Chloe. "Only a hundred times. You're very welcome."

"And I'm very thankful," she repeated.

Footsteps pounded down the stairway and Reed reappeared and sidled next to Chloe. "I have something I wanted to show you before you go pick up the girls." He turned to Morgan. "If you're free, I could use some help bringing it inside."

"I'm free." Technically his job was done, but it had been so many years since he'd spent time with the Texas Farradays he didn't mind lingering as long as he could.

With a nod, Chloe followed him and Morgan outside to one of the pick up trucks.

"I wanted you to tell us which room in the house to put it in." Watching her carefully, with the flick of a wrist, Reed removed the protective blanket from the piece of furniture underneath.

Chloe's mouth dropped open and her hands flew to her face. "Oh my."

"Do you like it?" Reed asked.

For some reason Morgan felt he was witnessing a private conversation and wondered if now would be a good time to check his boots for pebbles.

"Like it?" She swung around to hug him. "I love it. I don't think Nana's vanity ever looked this beautiful."

"I got a little help from Sam. Seems besides knowing cattle, the ranch foreman is pretty good with restoring antiques too. I followed his instructions and here you go."

Slowly her fingers trailed over the top, opened each of the slim drawers and then slid back across the top again. "I can't believe it. I thought it was ruined."

Reed shook his head without once removing his gaze from Chloe. Morgan had seen a lot of guys fall head over boot heels for a girl, but these two were so obviously in love with each other if Reed didn't put a ring on her finger and soon, he was a bigger fool than the guy on the hill.

Any minute now Morgan was sure they were going to self combust from staring at each other. "Shall we?" he dared to ask.

"Yes." Reed nodded. "Where do you want it, Chloe?"

"My room," she answered wistfully.

Good thing. Morgan wasn't looking forward to maneuvering that piece up the narrow staircase.

"We've got your bed all set up." Uncle Sean tightened one last screw on a piece they'd acquired from the loft and handed the tools over to Jamie. "They really don't make furniture like they used to."

"Tell me about it." Chloe eased herself onto the mattress. "I may need a ladder to get up here every night."

Laughter filled the room and Chloe's expression softened as she looked at Jamie. "I promise to give it a good home."

"Hey." He held his hands up, palms out. "I told you, you're doing me a favor. I have plans for that loft if I ever empty it out."

"That's what he says now." Uncle Sean slapped his nephew on the back, then lifting the tool box, stopped next to Morgan. "I don't know when we would have gotten this job done without your help."

"I'm only sorry Dad didn't say something to us sooner. I know slipping away from Mom is hard for him, but we take jobs out of town all the time. She never gave our taking a job away from home to help a veteran's widow a second thought."

"Next time we need help I'll remember to bypass my cousin."

"You do that." Morgan was so happy to be in the thick of things with his Uncle Sean and Brian's families that he easily fell into a man-hug with his uncle.

"All right." Aunt Eileen clapped her hands. "It's getting late. The house is looking fantastic, and the New Year's Eve party starts at Reed's at eight pm sharp so everyone get a move on."

Morgan laughed and his brother Quinn came up beside him. "I bet she could put Mom in her place."

"I bet she could put a platoon of Marines in their place." The two brothers grinned and followed everyone out the door. There was a party to attend.

The chatter and chaos that had taken over the ranch house reminded Morgan so much of growing up. His mom was the tough one, but his dad made sure the Irish spirit was in every aspect of their lives.

"Are you guys driving your own vehicles or riding with us?" Finn asked.

Ryan, the third brother who'd tagged along as part of the rebuilding crew, looked to Morgan and Quinn before answering. "We'll take one of our trucks."

Finn nodded. "Joanna and I are leaving in about fifteen minutes. Dad and Aunt Eileen may or may not be ready. If you guys are good to go, you can follow us."

"Sounds good."

Halfway out the door, Finn stopped and spun around. "Glad you guys are here." Without waiting for a response, he turned back and headed to his place.

"What the heck do you think happened all those years ago?" Quinn was asking himself as much as his brothers.

"I know what you mean. Mom always made it sound like we weren't welcome anymore, but I'm starting to think there's a rat in the well."

Morgan nodded. Something didn't smell right, but he wasn't going to let that start the New Year off on the wrong foot. The three flipped a coin to see who would drive and in less than an hour the three Farraday cousins strolled into a lovely brick ranch house.

"Welcome." Reed stretched out his hand to each brother. "There's punch in the kitchen and snacks around, but don't open the double doors please."

"Got it." Morgan had been to enough bachelor pads to know that every house had at least one room that started as a catch all and quickly grew into a storage unit.

Next the front door opened, blowing in a burst of cold air and two cowboys and their wives. Adam and Brooks stomped their feet at the mat almost in a synchronized beat.

"Hey," Adam said with a smile, foregoing the handshake and pulling Morgan into a hug. "I still can't believe y'all are here."

One by one the conversations for the night had shifted from insulation R factor and two by sixes to the growth in Tuckers Bluff, the coming additions of four more next generation Farradays, and how were they going to manage to keep Aunt Eileen's feet on the ground.

"I had a dream last night." Meg blinked. "Every time I asked our child what's the magic word, she answered Grandma."

Everyone within earshot burst out laughing. His uncle's new wife might be Aunt Eileen to most adults in the room, whether related by blood or not, but to the next generation she was Grandma.

The den had been set up as game night for the children. In order for the parents to have a good time, a couple of the Brady teens had been hired to baby-sit, but still different parents would wander in and out to check on their offspring. A few of Morgan's cousins wandered in just to play the games. It was easily turning into a magical start of a new year.

"Oh my heavens." Quinn bit down hard and practically moaned with delight. "Have you tasted these?"

"Which one is it?" Ryan asked.

"I think she said Mimosa."

"Oh yeah." Ryan smiled. "Reminds me of orange creamsicles."

"Oh hell no. These are way better."

Chloe came up to them with a tray of deviled eggs. "Try one?"

"Don't mind if I do," the three men echoed.

Adam, who was still standing chatting with his cousins, waved his hand. "Nope. I'm waiting for the meatballs. I heard Aunt Eileen made an extra big batch."

The conversation shifted from one delightful nibble to another and when it got to the stories of the two dogs, Morgan didn't know if he should laugh or take his cousin's temperature.

"He's not exaggerating." Sister, one of two interesting siblings who ran the local mercantile, shook her head at him. "Those dogs are special."

"And," Sissy, the other interesting sister, added, "I hear one gifted our Chloe a little something."

"I wouldn't go spreading any rumors now." Chloe appeared with a new tray in front of Adam. "I hear you're waiting on the meatballs."

"Oh, yes."

"Aren't you even a little curious?" Sissy asked.

Chloe shook her head. "Absolutely not."

But Morgan saw her gaze slip over to where Reed stood by the Christmas tree fidgeting with the contraption that had been playing Christmas carols all night. If Morgan didn't know better he'd swear the two were telepathic. No sooner did her gaze land on him than his eyes darted in her direction. Almost as if he knew she was looking at him. A silly smile took over his face and within seconds a grin to match bloomed on her lips. Oh, these two had it bad.

"Ooh." Aunt Eileen, who had been chatting with Catherine about plans for a nursery, backed into Morgan. "Sorry. That's my cue. Have to run."

Her cue?

"Did I miss something?" Quinn asked.

Morgan shrugged.

The next thing he knew, Aunt Eileen was sliding the pocket doors open. "Folks, I hope you've enjoyed the nibbles, but we've been saving the best for the New Year."

Morgan glanced at his watch. When had it gotten so late so fast? It was almost midnight already.

"In my family there are several traditions that we'd like to share with you. Of course we have lots of black-eyed peas on the dining room table." She smiled. "Though I can't claim that one, Texas had it before I got here."

The room burst into pockets of giggles. "There are grapes for good luck, and at exactly midnight we'll be opening the front door to let the year's blessings in and the back door to let the year's burdens out. And of course there's a basket of mistletoe sprigs. Anyone interested in finding their true love only need sleep with a sprig under their pillow tonight."

"Is it me," Quinn leaned into Morgan, "or is she suddenly developing an Irish lilt."

Morgan laughed. "Could be."

"Now everyone, time to help yourselves to a nice meal and

feel free to bang your bread on the wall if you so desire." Without explanation, she smiled and walked away from the dining room entrance.

Several heads turned to face each other, their brows buckled with confusion.

"You don't suppose Aunt Eileen is actually totally off her rocker and that's why Mom has kept us away all these years?"

Morgan scratched the top of his head. "Anything is possible, however unlikely, but I suspect if you Google the bread thing tomorrow, there's a reason."

"You're probably right."

"Of course I am." Morgan smiled and went in search of that good Irish food. It had been a hard push to finish out the punch list before Chloe arrived with all their belongings today. It had been important to him that she be able to start the New Year in her own house.

Already in the room, Chloe stood almost star struck, her fingers gently caressing the free space on the table. "This is *the* table."

Reed nodded. "It took some convincing, but I offered Jamie a fair price for it and since he didn't need it, he agreed."

"It's even prettier here than in the attic."

He nodded and swallowed hard.

Something was up. And even though the sound of sanity shouted for Morgan to leave these two alone, another part of him couldn't bring himself to move. Honestly, he wasn't sure he'd ever see so much love in such a small place ever again.

"I know you have lots of new plans for your house, your life," Reed started and Chloe lifted her chin to better see his face. "And I know the last several weeks have been a whirlwind of chaos, heartache, joy and excitement."

Slowly she nodded. Her expression blank, her eyes filled with hope.

"Why are you just standing in the entry—" Ryan came up beside him.

Stretching his arm out, Morgan cut his brother off. "Shh."

To his credit, Ryan silently glanced into the room and then saw what his brother had been watching and whispered, "Oh."

Reed dropped to one knee.

"And there it is," Morgan whispered with a smile.

"If you can see it in your heart to share those plans, your dreams, a home with me, whether in your house, or my house, or a new house all our own, you'd make me the happiest man in the world."

Morgan held his breath. She had to say yes.

From his pocket, Reed pulled out a velvet box and popped it open. "Will you marry me?"

The next second ticked by in extreme slow motion. Morgan's mouth went dry and Ryan's hand shot out to squeeze his arm. When Chloe flung her arms around Reed's neck, toppling them both over, repeating *yes,* Morgan shot up a fist pump and shouted a victorious woot. When applause erupted behind him, he realized he hadn't been the only one listening to the dining room table proposal.

"Looks like it's going to be another bumper crop year for love in Tuckers Bluff." A man Morgan hadn't met yet smiled beside him.

"Hi." Morgan shot his hand out. "Morgan Farraday, Sean and Eileen's nephew."

"Frank Carter," the man answered. "Cook at the Silver Spur."

"You're predicting a love-happy year?"

"No need to predict. More of a trend." The man spun about to face Morgan. "If you're looking for the love of your life to marry, just move to Tuckers Bluff."

Somehow, Morgan didn't think it was that simple. He glanced around at all his now married and happy cousins. A nice idea, but it couldn't possibly be that simple.

Excerpt from MORGAN

CHAPTER ONE

"I'll see you one and raised you two." Eileen Farraday tossed her chips onto the table. More chips clattered, landing in the makeshift pot. Her cards had been running hot all morning. She didn't dare move. Fear of her luck changing wouldn't even allow her to run to the ladies room. Grandma Siobaughn had always said, when your blessings are running high, don't change a thing. Well, that little saying was a two-way street. Her sainted grandmother was also known to get up and walk around while playing cards in order to change her luck for the better.

"Royal Flush." Flashing a huge grin, Ruth Ann fanned her cards out and waited triumphantly for the others to show their hands.

"Blast." Sally May slammed her cards down. "Thought you were bluffing."

So did Eileen. Who knew Ruth Ann would come up with one of the few hands that could beat her four kings.

"Oh my." Dorothy, one of the founding members of the Tuckers Bluff Ladies Afternoon Social Club, pointed over her cards to the front door.

Tall, slender, wearing shades almost as big as her face, and a hat well-suited for a glamorous star of a 1950's motion picture, a woman stood in the doorway of the café discretely scanning the room.

The well-dressed blonde reminded Eileen of her niece-in-law Meg the day she first came to Tuckers Bluff. Too pretty and too pressed to come from anywhere around these parts. "Wonder who she is."

"New school teacher?" Abbie suggested, holding out a coffee carafe, raising her brows at each of the ladies in silent question of more or not. "I heard she's due in town any day. Will be staying at Meg's B&B while she finds a permanent place."

"If she's the new elementary school teacher, I just celebrated my twenty-fifth birthday." Sally May skewered Abbie with a what-Kool-Aid-have-you-been-drinking glare. "No woman who works with young children on a daily basis shows up dressed like she fell off the cover of a Paris fashion magazine. Not even if she's *in* Paris."

"And especially not in dusty West Texas cattle country." Dorothy bobbed her head. "At the first sign of glue stick-y fingers or wayward Magic Marker, that woman would be running for home."

"Well, looks like we're fixing to find out." Eileen tipped her head in the direction of her niece-in-law Joanna coming through the door and greeting the newcomer. All Eileen would need was time to whip up a batch of her pumpkin brownies along with five minutes alone with Finn's wife and she'd have the whole scoop, including the stranger's blood type. *Yep. Curiosity wouldn't be killing this cat today.*

"Well, how about that." Dorothy faced the side window. "You may want to look at this, Eileen."

More interested in the newcomer, she dragged her gaze away from the two women still standing at the doorway and looked out the side window. Sitting at the edge of the parking lot, head tilted to one side, Gray, the beautiful wolf mix who now lived at the ranch, blinked at her. "What the heck is he doing all the way out here?"

"Maybe he stowed away in the back of your truck?" Ruth Ann suggested.

"Maybe." Her face pinched in thought. "But I don't think so."

"You don't suppose Gray's up to his old tricks again?" Sally May said softly.

All four heads turned to the tall blonde.

"Maybe." Eileen studied the newcomer carefully. *But for who?*

• • • •

Morgan Farraday carefully watched Meg's back as she stared at the columns of two by fours that until yesterday had been the rear wall of the small family living room. This morning had been spent ripping off the sheetrock and plaster from the only thing standing between the newly enclosed back porch and what would soon be an enlarged apartment for her and Adam's growing family.

"Wow, just wow." Meg spun and flung her arms around his neck, kissed his cheek, and practically bounced away from him to once again stare at the mostly open space. "This is going to be amazing."

"It's your vision." Morgan smiled at his cousin's wife. Meg was a smart and competent businesswoman who just happened to be a heck of a nice lady—and the perfect match for his cousin Adam. The delighted, wide-eyed gaze and grin that stretched from one side of her face to the other was the best affirmation of a well-executed plan. He loved making people happy, making a homeowner's renovation dreams come true. When the homeowner was family, all the better. "Now you'll have plenty of space for all of Fiona's things."

"Tell me about it. Who knew such a little bundle would come with so much…stuff." Chuckling, she continued to look at the newly opened space instead of facing him. "When do the studs come all the way down?"

"Now."

"Really?" Hands clasped tightly closed in front of her, she spun back around, somehow smiling even brighter than a moment before.

"New support beam is in place, we don't need these anymore. Want to help?"

"You sure?"

He held back a chuckle and pulling his hammer from the metal belt loop, grinning, he extended his arm. The next thing he knew, the studs were gone, Meg stood proudly admiring the truly spacious room, and heavy footsteps sounded behind them.

"Has anyone ever told you how sexy you look in a hardhat?"

"Can't say that I have." Morgan laughed at his cousin Adam ogling his wife as if they were still newlyweds. What was it with young love and this side of the family? These two made being in love look so easy. He'd learned a long time ago that aspirations and chaos eventually won out and life—his life—was much simpler on his own.

Meg rolled her eyes, removed her hat, and handed it over to Morgan. "Thank you. That was fun."

Fun? That had to be a first. He didn't know many women who enjoyed demolition. Another place and time and Morgan would have wondered if Meg had a single sister. Even if the construction business booming and pulling him all over the state, and like now, out of state, left no time for a woman in his life, he'd learned his lesson. Fool me once, shame on you, fool me twice, shame on me. Women as special as Meg simply didn't come along every day of the week. Not without strings. Complicated strings.

Moving closer to his wife, Adam curled his arm around her waist, drew her in and gently kissed her on the lips. "Seriously, you look great and so does the room."

Meg's eyes twinkled at her husband.

The simple exchange of love and affection felt oddly personal. Morgan shifted his gaze to the fallen studs, and examined them a short while before venturing to return his attention to his cousin and the now missing wall.

Meg patted her husband's arm and turned to Morgan. "I'm so glad you suggested the wall of windows instead of the typical double framed."

Her effervescent enthusiasm shoved his discomfort aside and once again reminded him why he was glad to be here. "When you mentioned how important light is to you, it was a no brainer."

"Looking good." Ryan, his brother closest in age, came in from the hall. "Soon you won't have to keep hauling Fiona all the way out to Uncle Sean and Aunt Eileen's to avoid the construction noise."

Meg squirmed in place. "Not so sure Aunt Eileen's going to like that, even if she let Becky have Fiona for a while so she wouldn't miss out on the card game."

Ryan shook his head. "Aunt Eileen really plays poker in a café?"

"Religiously." Adam chuckled.

"Well," Ryan shrugged, smiling and shaking his head, "only a few more days and we'll be out of your hair."

The light mood that had filled the room dimmed. Ever since doing the fire rehab on Chloe's house last Christmas, Morgan had been looking for a good reason to spend more than a weekend in Tuckers Bluff. When Adam had reached out to him explaining they didn't want to move out of the B&B but really needed some more space, Morgan and his brother jumped on the chance to come and stay at the ranch in the thick of this branch of the Farradays for a bit. Maybe he and Ryan shouldn't have worked so hard and fast.

The expression on Meg's face crumpled like a Sharpei. "I'll have you know we like having you two around. Besides, I'm not so sure Aunt Eileen is going like not having the baby every day, but she did mention that she wants to redo the master bath at the ranch. Says it's time for a walk-in shower."

"As a matter of fact," Adam waved a finger at him, "Brooks and Allison are almost ready to move forward with the next phase of the hospital."

Ryan chuckled. "Y'all wouldn't be trying to keep us in Texas, would you?"

"Yes," Adam and Meg echoed quickly.

Adam sidestepped his wife and nodded from one brother to the other. "It really has been nice having you guys around again." No doubt Adam was thinking about all the lost years between the two Farraday clans. Similar thoughts and feelings had passed over him since finding it so easy to pick up with his cousins exactly where they'd left off as teens.

"Don't look at us that way." Ryan shook his head. "It's been really great reconnecting. We'll be back more often, promise. Still, I can't shake this gnawing feeling that bringing us here to help out isn't a matter of supply and demand as much as a part of a masterful scheme of Aunt

Eileen's to marry off the only remaining Farraday bachelors."

Adam coughed and Meg thumped him lightly against the arm.

"What?" Adam shrugged at his wife. "The man could be right."

Smiling, Ryan shook his head more vigorously. "I'm glad all the married Farradays are so happy, really I am, but I happen to like being single. Able to go where I want when I want. Which reminds me." He turned to Morgan. "Owen and Pax are going hunting with a few guys this weekend. Think you can finish things up here without me?"

Arms crossed, Morgan nodded. He wasn't as anxious as Ryan to hurry home. Life had been good to him. Very good. Not once in recent years had he considered something was missing in his life. Until he'd returned to Tuckers Bluff, and even though he wasn't interested in any subversive matchmaking plots his aunt might have in mind, he still liked the idea of hanging around as long as he could.

"Yoo hoo," Becky called out.

The old saying about the pitter patter of little feet was absolutely true. Morgan turned at the female voice calling from downstairs and could hear the little footsteps rushing across the hardwood floors, no doubt making a bee-line for the stairs.

"Gotcha." DJ's voice carried up the stairs, followed by the giggles of their daughter Katie, officially Caitlin Helen Farraday.

All the adults on the third floor headed downstairs. The first person to reach the bottom, Meg retrieved her little girl from her sister-in-law's arms. Fiona and Katie, being only a couple of months apart, got along like the proverbial house on fire. It was a blast to watch those two side by side explore and discover the world around them. More fun than he would have thought a few short months ago.

"We may have to reconsider putting a gate on the first floor even if it's a bit inconvenient for guests." Adam shook his head at his niece doing her best to wiggle out of her father's arms.

"Don't do it on Katie's account. We're not here enough and before you know it, she'll be running up those stairs like an Olympic athlete without supervision." DJ set his girl down, the arm of a watchful parent prepared to launch if necessary to recapture the speed demon.

Expecting her to head straight for the lower steps again, Morgan was taken by surprise when instead Katie darted in his direction and threw her arms up at him.

"Well, hi there." After a few weeks with a passel of little ones, Morgan had gotten pretty comfortable with the routine. First, he'd play *whose belly is that,* tickling her tummy, then they'd do airplane, where he'd hold her over his head and zoom her back and forth until she giggled so loud that anyone in the room laughed along with them.

Where DJ's little Caitlin was the adventurous one, Adam's Fiona was the snuggler. Always happy to tuck her head into someone's shoulder and just watch and learn from the people around her, especially her cousin. Like right now. Eventually she'd give in to curiosity and take a turn with Uncle Morgan.

"You do that really well for a bachelor." Becky's sparkling eyes remained fixed on her daughter as Morgan held her high over his head.

"I catch on quick." He pulled Katie in close and rubbed her tummy with the top of his head. Her bursts of giggles had him and every other adult chuckling too.

His cousins had indeed found the true brass ring of life. Morgan had always been surrounded by family. He and his brothers were close, very close. He'd been content with that, but now he couldn't shake the feeling that he was missing out on something really special. Of course, he'd felt that way after college when he'd gone shopping for a ring for Carolyn, and look how well that had turned out.

• • • •

The hat was definitely overkill. Then again, so was the hot Texas sun. As a fair-haired kid with lily white skin growing up on the beaches of Southern California, it hadn't taken Valerie Moore long to learn the sun was definitely not on her side. Overstatement or not, hats were her friend.

"Valerie?" A petite, dark-haired woman with a smile as bright as the Texas sun looked up at her.

"Joanna?"

The woman stuck her hand out. "Welcome to Tuckers Bluff."

"Thank you." So far so good. Joanna was as pleasant in person as on the phone.

A waitress sidled up to Joanna sporting an equally bright grin. Coming from California, there was nothing unusual about everybody around you smiling, but these people all looked like Cheshire cats. Maybe it was the Texas heat.

"Well, this is a nice surprise." The waitress offered a quick hug.

"Hey." Jo returned the familiar embrace, turned and waved her arm to Val. "Valerie, this is my cousin-in-law,

Abbie."

"Nice to meet you." Abbie nodded.

"Pleasure," she responded, trying to add a little more oomph to her own smile.

"Since I'm in town, thought I might pop in later and visit with Brendan—and Jamie too, of course."

"Of course." The woman laughed. "If you go, make sure to check if he's home or taken the baby to the pub, though it's harder for Jamie to work now that Brendan is crawling."

Baby? At the pub? Val's gaze shifted from one woman to the other. Surely there had to be a good reason for a baby at a pub. Nothing came quickly to mind but she figured it had to be a doozy and then wondered if it was crazy enough to spin into a sitcom? Mentally shaking her head, she took a deep breath. Nobody liked a desperate producer. Too bad, the potential antics were starting to play in her head like a movie reel in fast motion.

"Everything okay?" Joanna asked her.

"What? Yes. Why?"

"You're shaking your head."

"Oh." Val laughed. Her expressions and gestures gave her thoughts away a few times too many. "Sorry, was thinking too hard."

"Ah." Joanna flashed that blinding Texas smile again.

"Table or booth?" Abbie grabbed a single menu.

"Booth. In the back."

"Got it." Joanna's cousin nodded and led them to a corner booth with a bit of distance between them and the nearest table, and handed Val a menu. "Things shouldn't get crowded for about another hour."

"Thanks."

It took a few moments to order drinks, establish that

Joanna, and just about everyone else in town, didn't need a menu, and settle into their seats before her phone buzzed and anticipation zinged through her system. "I have to take this. Will you excuse me?"

"Of course."

Weaving her way through the tables to the back hall in search of privacy, she passed a freestanding ladder, briefly considering who leaves an empty ladder in the middle of a hall. Phone to her ear, she debated ducking into the ladies room, but the way her luck had been running, every stall would be occupied and all would echo loudly when flushed at the same time. Turning her back to the dining area, she jammed a finger in her other ear and buried her face in the dark corner. "What did they say?"

Her best friend since freshman year at UCLA, and a screenwriter for one of the hottest serial adaptations on cable, Marilyn had used her connections to pitch this last idea. The hope had been that Val's efforts might get farther with an insider in her corner. "No go."

Crud. That's what she was afraid of. Her forehead thumped against the hard wall. Three series pitched, three series struck out. She couldn't blame them, she wasn't all that enthusiastic about the last project either, but getting out of the reality TV game was her best shot at a new full-time gig and moving her career to the next level. Too bad no one else thought so.

"You still there?"

"Yes."

"Sorry. Switching gears in this industry isn't easy."

Brother, did she know that. The question now was, even if she convinced Joanna to give her an option on the new book, if she couldn't get backing for anything but reality TV, what did it matter how good a story she brought to the table.

"They'd be interested if you come up with a fresh concept for a new home renovation show."

And again, wasn't that the problem? How many ways could a producer spin a married couple, any couple, fixing up old houses?

"That TV home remodel with all those retro stars was a hit. Maybe we should try something like that?"

"Then it wouldn't be fresh, would it?"

"This is Hollywood. Fake it."

"Easier said than done." If only she could fake her dwindling bank account. Lifting her head, she blew out a long, slow breath. "I'm at lunch. Let's talk later."

"Sounds good. Call when you get back to LA."

"Will do." Squeezing her eyes shut, she said a silent prayer. Her gut told her Joanna Farraday's book held the answer to all her problems.

Eyes open, she spun around, surprised by the blinding burst of light from a distant window. Taking a short step, she blinked and took another before her toe connected with something clunky. Her gaze dropped to the ground, still struggling to make out what was right in front of her. Who moved the ladder?

"Sorry." The voice was deep and low and very male.

Her gaze lifted. "No prob…" The words dried up in her mouth. Teetering on that once empty ladder, directly in her line of vision, perfectly rounded denim-clad masculine buns of steel came into *very* clear view. One muscular leg descended a step, pulling the denim more tightly against said steel buns. If she could have conjured up a drop of saliva she would have whistled.

"Excuse me," he rumbled.

Slowly her gaze dropped to his leather boot and back to that well-formed derriere and up to a state sized belt buckle.

"I need to get down."

Down? Once again, her focus wandered up and down before her brain finally began to fire on all pistons, realizing she was standing in his way. Taking a step back, her mouth connected with her brain. "I'm sorry. I didn't hear you come in."

"You were on the phone. It seemed important, but I only had a couple of minutes and I promised Abbie I'd take a look at the light."

"Yes." The single syllable wasn't quite the appropriate response, but the almost hypnotic timbre of his voice had veered her mind off track again. Stringing coherent words together wasn't going to happen.

On the ground, he slid a screwdriver into a pouch that hung from his hip. The way his hand rose to his forehead, she almost thought he was about to tip a nonexistent hat. "Thanks. Have a nice day."

A smile spread across his face, her gaze leveled with deep twinkling blue eyes, and for the second time in only a few short moments, her mouth went perfectly dry. Somehow she managed to mumble, *you too*, as he lifted the folded ladder and turned to walk away. The hammer and who knows what else jingled with every step he took. No wonder the network wanted a fixer upper show. She could binge watch that man at work any day.

MEET CHRIS

USA TODAY Bestselling Author of more than a dozen contemporary novels, including the award winning *Champagne Sisterhood*, Chris Keniston lives in suburban Dallas with her husband, two human children, and two canine children. Though she loves her puppies equally, she admits being especially attached to her German Shepherd rescue. After all, even dogs deserve a happily ever after.

More on Chris and her books can be found at
www.chriskeniston.com

Follow Chris on Facebook at ChrisKenistonAuthor
or on Twitter @ckenistonauthor

Questions? Comments?
I would love to hear from you.
You can reach me at chris@chriskeniston.com

CPSIA information can be obtained
at www.ICGtesting.com
Printed in the USA
BVHW031508150421
605033BV00004B/260